ROYAL COMBAT

(A play)

ILOMA CHIZOBA

EZU BOOKS LTD
ENUGU, NRI, ABUJA, CONNECTICUT

First Published 2010 by

EZU BOOKS LTD.
22 Lumumba Street
New Haven, Enugu
Tel: +2348033425625
        +2348025067944
E-mail: regolum@y.mail.com
Website: www.ezubooks.blogspot.com

Typeset by: Solomon Scripts
Tel: 08035499445   E-mail: solomazoba@yahoo.com

Cover Design and Concept: Rowland Egolum and Che Stanley.

To the memories of

My Grandmothers

MRS. RHODA ILOMA (*Nee Dimejesi*)

and

MRS. EGOABUNWA UMEALAJEKWU (*Nee Oforkansi*) who died on 9th December, 2006 and in 1993 respectively.

&

My Mentor
PROFESSOR DANIEL I. ILEGA who died on 21st August, 2008.

CAST

Igwe Ezeilo, King of Umuezeka
Lolo Olachi, Queen of Umuezeka
Ikenga, son of Ezeilo and Olachi
Ichie Onuoha
Ichie Ononankume
Ichie Udokasi
Nze Akubuike   Members of King's Cabinet
Nze Okwudiri
Nze Eluwa
Atinga, Royal head servant
Otikpo
Isiaboncha   King's Bodyguards
Omenala, Agunu Chief Priest
Akpuruka, a drunkard
Ifeuwabunike, Olachi's uncle
Ashimeleze, Olachi's brother
Opuruiche, mother of Chimaobi and Nnaemeka
Chimaobi, son of Opuruiche
Nnaemeka, brother of Chimaobi
Commander, leader of assassins
Onuma, one of the assassins
Debe, last child of *Ichie* Onuoha

Townspeople, Servants, Singers, Drummers, Dancers, Flutist, Town Crier, Spokeswoman, Demonstrators etc.

PROLOGUE

A voice is heard
Yelling in throe of childbirth
Thy pain of conception will multiply
In sorrow thou shall reproduce
Another voice is heard
Squeaky, less bitter
A child is born
First issue of the royal couple
Ezeilo and Olachi
Igwe and *Lolo* of Umuezeka

In a split second, all in Umuezeka and environ inhale fresh air of the good news that diffuse into atmosphere.

Townspeople are happy, singing and dancing to drumbeats. Cavorting and rejoicing are the order of the day. Jubilation sprints through the length and breadth of Umuezeka's geography and beyond. People troop to the palace, both old and young - it is an elated crowd.

Symbolic sounds, the dexterous and vivacious flutist produces, chime in perfectly with the drumbeats. Later, he *dolce* plays solo. The door of the *obi* cracks open, the refulgent curtain drawn aside.

Olachi is in front. Happiness is written all over her appealing face. Who wouldn't be? She tries to join the performing girls wiggle her waist, but is too weak and exhausted for that profitable bodily exercise. She is accompanied by *Umuada*. One of them is painstakingly carrying the baby as if she is holding an eagle's egg.

The Prince is clad in royal blue velvet and adorned with a roseate cap and purple bangle.

Ezeilo in his ravishing royal regalia and insignia of crown cum scepter enters the palace reception room gleefully. Behind him, his bodyguards hold their machetes with stretched out arms as if about to chop off their Master's head.

Following is the King's cabinet – the *Ichies* and *Nzes*. They walk in, preening their fineries and piercing the floor with their scepters, which produce sounds that strike a chord with the drumming, like an icing sugar to a cake.

Youths of royalty are at the rear. It was a blossom celebration, a palace of praise. The boys' bass voices couple with the vibration of the girls' legs and rumps nearly spoilt the floor modishly plastered with crude mud. As for the children, they struggle to feed their eyes by peeping through the wooden windows – all for one child.

> First of the King and Queen
> After a decade of wedlock
> Male for that matter
> Priceless Prince of the Palace
> Heir to the throne
> Their next *Igwe*

The King sits on his rococo throne and his entourage took their seats in turns. They fan themselves gorgeously, while Atinga fans Ezeilo with veneration.

As they are all sat, the artistes dive obstreperously into showmanship. Each strut his or her stuff. When the bard took center stage; being accompanied by smooth tunes of the endowed flutist, the King and his cabinet could not help rising to their feet and showcase briefly royal dance steps which are rarely displayed or seen.

The people stand in cult and gaze in awe. They take their seats and the singers resume the carnival. Drinks and food are being served. People fill their stomachs while the dancers seethe the treat.

Suddenly Omenala appears and the lively palace becomes a graveyard. His presence is quite unexpected and novel. The boss-eyed Agunu Chief Priest stands for a while at the entrance and walks straight to the King. They exchange pleasantries.

Never had Omenala attended a social gathering especially when uninvited. Never had he also moved alone. He lives in Agunu forest, kilometers away from Umuezeka dwelling places. Yet from such distance, the people of Umuezeka feel his preternaturalness.

What must have made Omenala, the awesome Chief Priest of Agunu, to leave his abode, the shrine in the thick forest, to the King's palace all alone? This preoccupies the thoughts of everyone especially the elders and the King who know very well his routine and style. Whatever it is, it must be grave.

Omenala breaks the silence and releases them from the chains of suspense.

OMENALA: You all offend the gods with your merry making. Rejoicing for a harbinger of doom?

All are motionlessly transfixed, hearing Omenala's strange words.

OMENALA: [*Pointing at the baby who Olachi is now fondling*]. This boy will be brave, but will be killed by a strong and powerful man who doesn't want him to become the next *Igwe*.

Everyone shouts *Aru*. Omenala perforates the mud floor with his staff, and exit. Singers, dancers, drummers; all are now forlorn.

Oh! A bad fortune
An ominous future
Mission of tragedy and demise
Should be nipped

Mother weeps
Father thunderstruck
Townspeople mourn
Trees listen

Dancers and flutist cease performing
Drummers down in the dumps
Singers groan
Dirge fills the air

Women console Olachi
She refuses to be – frenetic
Tears drizzle
Wetting the floor

Father shouts, "No! No!! No!!!
Not the first fruit of my loins
After ten years of patience
Not in Umuezeka"

Children run to their homes
Slamming doors with towering velocity
As if hounded by spirits
Scenery, kerfuffle

Chiefs shaking their heads, exeunt
Umuada walk away sorrowfully

Youths stroll away listlessly
Leaving the unfortunate royals

It is joy turned grief
Sorrowful day for Umuezeka
Orchestration of mortar and pistol
Unheard that night

Misery, the royals' present guest
None to commiserate
Ezeilo consoles
But she could not bear it

"My son, quench like a candle in the
wind?
Who would propel that evil wind?
Deserves death, painful slow one
Shred in pieces"

Baby cries
Mother carries him inside
Leaving Ezelio
Alone in the woeful world of worry

ACT ONE

SCENE 1

The next day, Ezeilo wakes up very early walking aimlessly in his palace. He and his wife couldn't sleep. More also as the baby cried spasmodically till dawn.

After some minutes of pensive walk, Ezeilo stands with arms akimbo, looking upwards as if communicating telepathically with celestial beings.

EZEILO: [*Back from seeming soul travel*]. Guards!

BODYGUARDS: [*Prostrate*]. O King, live forever!

EZEILO: [*To Otikpo*]. Call the Queen for me.

OTIKPO: Yes your Highness. [*Enters inside*].

EZEILO: [*To Isiagboncha*]. Bring my seat and another for the Queen.

ISIAGBONCHA: Yes your Highness. [*Enters inside*].

Isiagboncha comes out with the *Igwe*'s seat. He is quickly followed by Otikpo, who is carrying a smaller seat. The royal chair is sophistically embellished with ormolu and carvings.

Ezeilo is still standing even after being informed of the presence of his throne.

OLACHI: [*Comes out sluggishly*]. My lord! [*Sits sorrowfully*].

EZEILO: [*Turns and take his seat*]. Ola-a please don't kill yourself because of the child's proclaimed bad luck. See how emaciated you have become overnight and how reddish your eyeballs are. Crying will do you no good.

OLACHI: [*Gestures painfully*]. What else do you want me to do? You know what we've been through all these years. Now this one has come, they are saying he will die untimely. Oh, my baby! [*Sobs*].

EZEILO: [*Consolingly touch her shoulders*]. It's okay. I know. He is my son too, my first child. But tears don't raise the dead or stop death from coming. [*Pause*]. Nevertheless, something must be done.

[*Stands energetically in a mean mood*]. The innocent boy cannot just die like that. Moreover, we are not getting any younger. [*Looks straight ahead*]. No one knows when the next bunch of breadfruit will fall. This one that has fallen would not be thrown to the goats without getting out the seeds.

My child would not die like an outcast; or like the son of a coward. No! Never! Not without a good fight as long as I, King Ezeilo 1 of Umuezeka lives.

OLACHI: [*Cleans her tears with the edge of her wrapper*]. My lord, what will you do? [*Ezeilo hesitates*]. Please tell me.

EZEILO: I don't quite figure it out now. In fact, I am a bit confused.

Olachi is thrown deeper into the cliff of glumness. She walks inside sobbing. Ezeilo likewise, was too downcast to console her.

As he sat contemplating, the *Ichies* and *Nzes* walk in. Empathy and sorrow could be seen written on their faces.

CHIEFS: May you live forever O King!

EZEILO: [*Sits up*]. You are all welcomed.

Guards enter inside and come out with one bench each, and situate them opposite each other.

ONUOHA: [*Speaks on behalf of others*]. *Igwe*, I greet you. [*Bows, while Ezeilo nods*]. Respected elders of Umuezeka, I salute you.

CHIEFS: We salute you too.

ONUOHA: We have come not to sympathize, but to empathize with you *Igwe* concerning our Prince. Because we believe that your problem is our problem, just as ours is yours.
However, our people say prompt action forestalls bad unforeseen event. Consequently, we have come to know what you intend doing and possibly rub minds with you on what should be done. [*Facing his fellow Chiefs*]. Do I speak your minds? [*They nod their heads in concord*].

ONONANKUME: *Ichie* Onuoha has in fact hit the nail on the head. Since we know the words of our gods are irrevocable, we should start now to look for the black goat before it gets dark.

UDOKASI: *Igwe*, may your days be long.

EZEILO: May it be well with thee.

UDOKASI: Elders of our land, I greet you.

CHIEFS: We greet you too.

UDOKASI: When oil touches one finger, it extends to the rest. *Igwe*, whatever happens to you has also happened to the entire people of Umuezeka. Therefore, you should endeavour to do something in order to avoid the impending ordeal. [*Sits*].

Ezeilo calmly seated and morose, did not respond to their provocative speeches.

AKUBUIKE: [*Stands*]. My fellow elders I greet you. We cannot sit here and watch the great town of Umuezeka go into extinction. From what Omenala said; he will be murdered when he is about to replace you as the next *Igwe*, of course at your death. This means that we will have no King and no hope of getting one. Because he will not be married, neither will he have offspring, since our Kings choose their wife at their coronation. And you know what? We will become like herd without shepherd.

CHIEFS: [*In unison*]. May, our gods forbid.

AKUBUIKE: [*Continues with his dreaded analysis*]. Then our enemies will easily destroy or subject us to scorching servitude. I mean *ohu*.

The Chiefs sigh noisily. With their hands, they make circles above their heads, producing a sharp sound with their thumbs and middle fingers.

EZEILO: My honourable Chiefs, I thank you all for your concern. But what do you want me to do? [*Gestures*]. Yes, the words are from the gods; they are inexorable. But the child is still a baby.

OKWUDIRI: Elders of our land I salute you.

CHIEFS: We salute you.

OKWUDIRI: May you live long, *Igwe*! We don't have to wait till he is grown. Now is the right time. Don't forget no king of

Umuezeka will have two sons of the same age range alive, because of what happened between the two sons of your uncle. How the second killed the first because of inordinate ambition to rule, and how the ghost of the first haunted him till he died mysteriously. Then their father committed suicide, after which your father took over the mantle of leadership and you, replaced him at his death.

Now, who knows what is in the offing that prompted the gods to reject this child. [*Enunciates*]. It is better we kill him now, so that you can have another heir. [*Sits*].

EZEILO: [*Twitch*]. What! You must be mad.

OKWUDIRI: Me? Mad?

EZEILO: Yes. You must have gone off your gourd for suggesting I kill my child, my first son, just like that?

OKWUDIRI: Anyway, that is your own kernel to break. I am only trying to   help.

EZEILO: [*Vexed*]. You hear that rudeness. Are you all sitting quiet, and watch your King insulted?

UDOKASI: I pray you *Igwe*, don't be angry. Sit, let's discuss this issue amicably and come to a consensus. It's very critical.

EZEILO: [*Yell of regal rage*]. Sit and discuss what? My child's crucifixion, isn't it? Oh, you are in support?

UDOKASI: Ah! I am not.

EZEILO: You are not? Okay.

Olachi enters.

OLACHI: What is the matter my lord?

EZEILO: [*Pointing at Nze Okwudiri*]. Is this idiot, telling me -

OKWUDIRI: [*Interjects*]. You see how the *Igwe* openly insults me.

EZEILO: Why won't I? You hard hearted animal.

OLACHI: Calm down, your blood is hot.

EZEILO: Why won't it be? Since grey hairs can't offer wise suggestion other than ask me to kill – [*Halts spontaneously*].

OLACHI: Kill? Kill who?

Ezeilo hesitates while her anxiety soars to the firmament. He refuses to answer because he knows it will sadden her greatly. But putting one and two together, coupled with the consensus dumbness of the proposing elders and her opposing husband; she deciphers that the lamb debated over for slaughter is her only child. She runs inside crying.

> The couch hosts bouts of weeping
> Soaked with tears
> Floor bore her angry stamps
> Rancorous cries reverberates inside

EZEILO: [*Anger mixed with bitterness*]. You see what you have caused? You see. [*Pointing at Nze Okwudiri*]. Look let me tell you, if anything happens to my child, I will hold you responsible and make sure you suffer till you die, rotten swine!

[*Okwudiri sighs*]. You hear that. You hear that treachery. He is really against me. May *arusi-odum* visit you in his time, you disloyal and heartless beast?

All is speechless and afraid of the King's towering wrath, including Okwudiri. No one dare to intervene so as not to get a red card of enmity, especially with the mention of *arusi-odum*, the most dreaded god of Umuezeka.

EZEILO: Go, go, you all.
ONUOHA: [*Astonished*]. You are chasing us away from the palace?
EZEILO: Is it your inheritance? I say leave. Go and kill your sons.

The Chiefs feeling grossly humiliated exeunt. Ezeilo goes inside, consoles his wife, while the Bodyguards carry the benches inside.

SCENE 2

Ezeilo is seated on his throne. He is very worried and apparently in dilemma. The Bodyguards seem also not to be at rest but not like the vexed Ezeilo.

EZEILO: [*Soliloquize*]. Kill my son? My only child? After ten years of marriage?

Never! Never, I say. It won't happen. I will rather massacre all the strong men in Umuezeka. [*Cogitates*]. Yes. It is better than killing an innocent child who has done nothing to be condemned to death. At least the men have sons who will perpetuate their names. [*Vows*]. May I not live to see him slain like an orphan. [*Molding courage*] A warrior is always a warrior, no matter what. As for that simpleton who calls himself Okwudiri, he can rejoice in *ofia ekabo*.

This self-talk seems to have positive effect on Ezeilo's emotional state, which was festered by yesterday's abusive imbroglio.

EZEILO: [*Calls*]. Atinga. [*No response*]. Atingaaa.

ATINGA: [*Rushes out*]. Yes your Highness [*Genuflects*].

EZEILO: Must I incur a hoarse voice before you answer?

ATINGA: [*Bows*]. I'm sorry your Highness.

EZEILO: You better be. Call the Queen.

ATINGA: [*Nods*]. Right away your Highness. [*Vamoose and comes out almost immediately*]. *Igwee!* [*Bows his head*]. Here I am.

EZEILO: Did I send for you? Where is she?

ATINGA: She sleeps your Highness

EZEILO: Sleep?

ATINGA: Yes your Highness. Far, far beyond *obizi.*

EZEILO: [*Irritated*]. Shut your trap, you slaphappy fellow. Did I ask how far she has slept or have you ever gone beyond *obizi?*

ATINGA: I am sorry your Highness.

EZEILO: Sorry always evaporates your mouth like vapour. [*Dismisses him*]. Go. [*Atinga disappears*].

When Ezeilo could no longer wait for Olachi, he decides to have a rest too. After having siesta, they came out together sleepily.

Ezeilo places his right hand across the delicate shoulders of Olachi, whose face is pretty synonymous in context with feces that just received a catapult shot.

EZEILO: I have told you times without number to stop crying. You cry too often and scantily eat. Look at how emaciated you've become. I don't feel happy seeing you cry and worn out, like a woman mourning her dead husband. [*Emotional*]. You don't know how every drop of your tears sink deep down in my heart.

OLACHI: [Supports her jaw]. It is because you are a man that is why you don't cry as I do.

EZEILO: Yes, I am a man. But a woman should not cry herself to death. And who told you that men don't cry? [*Yawns*].

OLACHI: Why yawn so heavily?

Ezeilo yawns again.

OLACHI: You must be hungry my lord. Let me get you something to eat.

EZEILO: Please do.

Olachi goes inside the kitchen and after a while comes out with food on a tray. She is accompanied by a female and male servant. They are carrying a bowel, a cup of potable water and a dwarfish table.

OLACHI: Here is your food my lord.
EZEILO: Thank you my dear.

The manservant positions the table in front of Ezeilo while Olachi drops the food on it. The maid drops gently the cup of water and kneels with the bowel of water in her hands, while Ezeilo washes his hands. When the King is through, she keeps the bowel beside the table and joins the other servant inside.

The ball is now in *Igwe* Ezeilo's court. The whistle is blown. Ezeilo strategizes the ball quickly, being goal-hungry. Given that, there is neither a goaltender nor defenders, the goal post conceded a lot of goals. The equally goal-hungry spectators watch freely without cheering the goal-scorer, probably because his balls were terrifyingly big, big as his child's pate.

Igwe Ezeilo ate hungrily, forgetting his wife. It was not until towards the end of second half, that he remembered her.

EZEILO: Ah, come and join me.
OLACHI: Thank you, I have eaten already.
EZEILO: [*Exploring the fish and meat dotted soup*]. Okay, if you say so. [*Comments*]. The food is very delicious.

Olachi smiles. Nothing makes a woman so happy than when her husband cherishes her food and acknowledges it. This is a vital factor in marriage as some women have been sent packing for bad meals.

Ezeilo coughs suddenly; pepper seems to have gone the wrong way.

OLACHI: Sorry my lord. [*Gives him the cup of water*].
EZEILO: [*Drinks and gets relieved*]. The pepper is cursed. It nearly made me shout like your baby. [*Both laugh*].
OLACHI: You better stop laughing, before the pepper makes you cry like your child.

EZEILO: [*Halts eating and laughs loudly. Olachi joins him*]. I am satisfied.

OLACHI: Are you sure? Or is it because of the pepper?

EZEILO: Not at all. My stomach is filled. Even, someone who has ulcer would eat this food to his full despite the pepper. Ask me why?

OLACHI: [*Smiling*]. Why?

EZEILO: [*Enunciates*]. Because it is superb.

OLACHI: Thank you my lord.

EZEILO: Is alright. [*Pointing at the bowl of water*]. Give me the water.

Olachi collects the bowl of water beside the table for her husband to wash his hands. When he is through, Olachi calls Atinga to tidy the table. Atinga comes in, and takes away the tray of plates, cup and bowl.

OLACHI: [*Calls*]. Atinga. Atinga

EZEILO: Why are you calling him?

OLACHI: The table.

EZEILO: [*Looks at the petty center table*]. What about it?

OLACHI: He didn't take it away.

EZEILO: [*Sighs*]. Sometimes, I wonder what kind of chief servant he is.

ATINGA: [Comes out]. Yes, her Highness.

OLACHI: Come here. [*Atinga draws near in fear*]. Why did you leave this table? Must I tell you everything, one by one before you do it? Don't you have common sense?

ATINGA: [*Bits his finger*]. I forgot your Highness.

OLACHI: One day you will forget your head at home and go to the market.

EZEILO: [*Complements his wife*]. He only delights in making stupid pranks.

OLACHI: Don't worry my lord; I will start dealing with him. Oh, you are still standing there looking at me. [*Moves to him and draws his ear*]. *Ngwa,* carry the table naughty boy. *Ngwa,* move stupid boy [*Still drawing his ear; both exeunt*].

ACT TWO

SCENE 1

The King and his wife slept well last night. After washing his face, he went to his *obi*. There he took a nap while his Bodyguards were at work. Suddenly, Ezeilo sits up like one who had a bad dream, picks his scepter and pins it on the floor. His Bodyguards shudder.

EZEILO: [*Soliloquize*]. Sacrifice my son? I know the words of Omenala are not to be jettisoned or trivialized, but what if I obey and the people of Umuezeka are left without a King? No! He must live. After all, sometimes in men's history, there is twist of fate; more also when the gods seem to be inconsiderate. [*Takes in and releases deep breath*]. Isiagboncha.

ISIAGBONCHA: [*Bows*]. Your Highness.

EZEILO: Call the Queen.

Isiagboncha executes the errand. Minutes later, Olachi comes out.

OLACHI: Yes my lord. [*Wears a brighter look*].

EZEILO: [*Admires Olachi*]. Wow! You look like Agbonma.

OLACHI: [*Smiles broadly*]. Is she not a woman like me?

EZEILO: That's true. You have a point.

OLACHI: [*Flattered*]. Thank you all the same. [*Sits*].

EZEILO: Now I know why you look so beautiful.

OLACHI: Why?

EZEILO: The attire you are putting on.

OLACHI: Is it because you bought it for me? If the shape is not there, [*demonstrates*] how will the attire fit in?

EZEILO: [*Laughs*]. Well, having a good shape is one and wearing a nice cloth is another, but you know what?

OLACHI: What?

EZEILO: None adds a morsel of pounded yam to my stomach. [*Both laughs*].

OLACHI: [*Still laughing*]. You are funny.

This fun talk seems to improve the psychological state of Olachi.

EZEILO: [*Alters tone*]. Olachi.

OLACHI: Yes my lord.

EZEILO: I called you because of the child.

OLACHI: [*Countenance changes*]. Our son?

EZEILO: Yes. Go and get him.

Olachi loses her voice looking at her serious Ezeilo.

EZEILO: I said go and get the child or you don't hear anymore?

Olachi stands, walks halfway and turns back, looking at his determined husband. *What does he want to do with the child? Why so desperate and stern? Or has he suddenly succumbed to the pressure of the Chiefs? May I not live to see that happen,* she reasons within her. Olachi enters the bedroom and comes out with the child. A zebrine cloth is wrapped around his buttocks. Beads are on his waist, wrist and ankle.

EZEILO: Here you are [*Drops his scepter and carries the child*]. Nwa oma, ebubedike, *nwa ge je mgba, onye ga achi obodo Umuezeka.*

Olachi migrates from one stage of puzzlement to another as Ezeilo eulogizes his son. *What are these big names for?*

EZEILO: This is your father calling. [*Baby cries*]. Don't cry. Your father is the one carrying you. [*Baby cries louder*].

OLACHI: I think he is hungry. He wants breast milk.

EZEILO: If that's why he is crying, then go and give it to him.

Ezeilo gives the baby to Olachi and to Ezeilo's surprise, he calms down. Mother and child: super-bond. Olachi walks inside the living room with the baby.

SCENE 2

After a long time of breast-feeding, Olachi enters and meet Ezeilo and his guards having a swell time.

OLACHI: [*Kicks Isiagboncha*]. You are sleeping? Otikpo, you too?

Bodyguards rise to their feet.

OTIKPO: We are alert. [*Suspends his machete in the air*].
OLACHI: [*Irritated*]. Okay. [*Taps Ezeilo*]. My lord. Eze, wake up.
EZEILO: [*Jerks up*]. Where is the baby?
OLACHI: [*Taken aback*]. Ah, what is it? Were you dreaming of him?
EZEILO: I am very much alert. Where is he?
OLACHI: He is inside sleeping.
EZEILO: Then this is the right time.
OLACHI: For what? [*Anxious and curious*].
EZEILO: [*Hotly*]. Go and get the child. [*Pointing at her*] And no more questions.
OLACHI: [*Thinking that Ezeilo wants to do something unpleasant*]. The child is asleep.

EZEILO: You provoke me woman! For the last time, go and get the child.

Olachi being aware of her husband's depth of wrath; enters and comes out with the baby, with her heart in her mouth.

EZEILO: That's better. [*Carry the child while Olachi stands and watch*]. A good wife should respect, absolutely respect her husband. So obey first before asking questions.
Why I ask for the child is for us to join heads together and choose a nice name for him, that's all. And instead of complying, you became headstrong, like a child who refuses to fetch water for his mother, because she did not allow him play.

OLACHI: [*Remorseful and relaxed*]. Forgive me my lord. I never knew that was why you asked.

EZEILO: It's alright. Sit. So, what name do you propose?

OLACHI: [*Smiling and contemplating simultaneously. She articulates one*]. Ndubuisi.

EZEILO: No, my dear! It doesn't sound royal. He shall be called Ikenga - bundle of strength. Isn't it a good one?

OLACHI: It's okay, my lord.

EZEILO: Then henceforth, Ikenga is your name. [*Lifts him up*]. Ikenga, son of Ezeilo, King of Umuezeka.

OLACHI: [*In high spirit*]. It's wonderful. My lord, I think we should invite friends and townspeople to celebrate his naming ceremony.

EZEILO: [*Provoked*]. Invite which friends? What concerns the people when I give my son a name?

Olachi frowns. Ezeilo carrying Ikenga walks gradually away from the Queen, while his Bodyguards as usual escort him. Olachi follows him swiftly to know where he is going and what he intends to do.

EZEILO: [*Yells*]. Go back and sit. Alright, come if you want the gods to strike you mad.

OLACHI: [*Halts*]. Please whatever you do, don't stain your palms. [*Ezeilo stops, staring at her*]. Yes, the gods are not to be underestimated, but sometimes when taken too seriously makes one a ready instrument of fulfilling their prophecy, so said my father.

Ezeilo angrily turns his back to Olachi and approaches the ancestral royal shrine. Olachi helplessly looks on till they are out of sight.

Igwe enters with his back, while the guards wait outside facing the north. He makes some incantation and lays Ikenga in between some scary objects of divination. He collects some palm leaves strangely knitted with a gewgaw. Deeps it in an old calabash full of thick green water and pastes it thrice on Ikenga's squeaky-clean temple. Then he lacerates the skin close to each of the green dots with his penknife.

I, Uduenyi Ezeilo, Igwe Umuezeka
Nkenke ehi na chu Igwe ehi oso
Custodian of royal sanctuary

Leader of your people
Greet you with stretched out arms
Arusi-odum, god of war and life
Protector of all males
I salute you
Your son is in your abode
He has been given a royal name
Ikenga, sack of strength
You have heard it
May it be acceptable to you
Odum, I greet.

King Ezeilo comes out the way he entered, and calls his Bodyguards aside.

EZEILO: [*Speaking in low pitch*]. I suppose you know the fate of the Prince.

BODYGUARDS: Yes, your Highness.

EZEILO: Now I want you to do something for me.

BODYGUARDS: Your wish is our command, your Highness.

EZEILO: That's good. [*Beckons them closer*]. Go, summon all the powerful men in Umuezeka. Tell them the King wants to see them immediately at the evil forest.

If they ask why, tell them for urgent security reason. And if they ask why the evil forest, tell them due to how confidential it is; the King does not want eavesdropping – the walls you know have holes.

[*Hands them a bag of cowries*]. Give them this, so that they may follow you without delay. When you reach the entrance of the evil forest, separate yourself from them and some men will do their job. Take the bag of money; give it to the men and run back home. Don't look back. Is that understood?

BODYGUARDS: [*Amazed and somewhat frightened*]. Yes your Highness.

EZEILO: Let me warn you. Don't allow anybody notice you. Is that clear?

BODYGUARDS: Yes, your Highness.

EZEILO: You can go now.

Isiagboncha and Otikpo look at each other and disappear. Ezeilo looks around and return to his *obi*. He finds Olachi still waiting.

EZEILO: You are still seated here?

OLACHI: Yes my lord. You stayed so long.

EZEILO: [*Didactically*]. You don't rush when you talk to the gods. [*Gives her Ikenga*]. You may go inside.

OLACHI: [*Walks halfway inside and turns*]. What of Otikpo and Isiagboncha?

EZEILO: I sent them on an errand; they will be back soon.

OLACHI: Okay. Let me have a nap with the baby.

EZEILO: That's good. I will join you soon. [*Olachi enters inside. Ezeilo speaks to himself*]. It is the only way out; my only recourse; the only way to save my son. [*Sits, shaking his legs anxiously*].

Hours later, Isiagboncha and Otikpo rush inside panting.

EZEILO: What happened? [*Looks around*] Was it done?

Bodyguards nod. Ezeilo smiles in accomplishment.

EZEILO: Now let me see that powerful man that will kill my son. [*To his Guards*]. Promise me you will keep what you saw secret.

The Guards acquiesce. But to be sure of their loyalty, he made them take an oath. As King Ezeilo retires, the eyes of the Bodyguards meet in suspicious silence.

SCENE 3

In the King's palace, the *Ichies* and *Nzes* are seated in peck order. Except for the conspicuous absence of Okwudiri, they are seated in perfect pairs. As they chitchat, the door cracks open and the King flanked by his Bodyguards enters.

CHIEFS: [*Bows*]. O King, may you live forever!
[*All standing while Igwe Ezeilo sits*].
EZEILO: Have your seats.

After some seconds of silence, *Igwe* broke the ice unfriendly.

EZEILO: What is it that brought you to my palace, which could not wait till the cock crows the third time? I hope it is not something pertaining to my son, otherwise you better leave.

ONUOHA: Not at all. [*Stands*]. Our fathers use to say, when the King and elders of the land are not united, the entire town is in trouble and prone to invasion. So we deemed it necessary to come and amicably sort things out with you. As a matter of fact we have not come to talk about your son who is also our son, [*looks at his colleagues for support, which they readily grant by nodding their heads*] but to seek peace.

EZEILO: Then, ensue it.

ONONANKUME: I think kola; our symbol of peace is required.

ELUWA: Yes, *Ichie* Ononankume is right. Our forefathers use to say, a good child washes his face and mouth in the morning before he runs to his mother for food.

AKUBUIKE: And a man, who hears a new song in his house or compound, should at least jump if he doesn't know how to dance to the rhythm.

Ezeilo, knowing the destination of these proverbs beckons Otikpo to get kola nuts. Minutes later, Otikpo comes out with a saucer of kola nuts. He places it on a stool in the midst of the elders and goes back to his duty post.

EZEILO: [*Endeavours to be polite*]. Elders of our land, here is kola.

ONUOHA: *Nnhu. Ugbua ka ibiara.* Thank you very much *Igwe*. The rat is in my house again, my fellow elders. I have to chase it or do I leave it?

ALL: No. [*In unison*].

UDOKASI: You have to chase it away; else it would cause domestic havoc. [*Laughter reigns supreme*].

ELUWA: You may kill it if you wish.

Ichie Onuoha collects a kola nut and removes his feathered cap.

ONUOHA: *Alaja-Umeh,* this is kola from the King. May it be well with him, if it comes from his heart. If not, thou god of kola nut trees and fertility knows best. [*Ezeilo stares at him*]. But we know and believe that a father will not poison his heir or give his son stone in lieu of bread. As we have this kola, may we have life -.

ALL: *Isea!*

ONUOHA: We will chew it, and chew long life.

ALL: *Isea!*

ONUOHA: As we chew this kola, we will have both males and females.

ALL: *Isea!*

ONUOHA: We will live to see them grow and see their children's children.

ALL: *I-s-e-a* [*Some nod their heads*].

ONUOHA: We will not bury them, but they will bury us.

ALL: *Ise-a.*

ONUOHA: As we hold this kola, we hold peace. And may the peace reign in   our hearts.

ALL: *Isea!*

ONUOHA: In our homes.

ALL: *Isea!*

ONUOHA: In the King's palace.

ALL: *Isea.*

ONUOHA: And in our beloved land – Umuezeka.

ALL: *Ise-aaa! [Pierce the earth with their scepters].*

ONUOHA: *[Breaks the kola nut].* This has four strands. *[Bends and draws four hollow lines on the ground]. Orie, Afor, Nkwo, Eke, [Puts each piece inside the hollow lines and made them invisible with sand]* that is yours. *[Takes another whole kola nut and throws it outside]. Alaja-Umeh,* that's yours. *[Takes another and throw it outside, but not as far as the former]. Arusi-odum,* take yours. *[Takes yet another, breaks it and pour them in their midst].* Our ancestors have yours. And may the tree of this kola nut never dry up.

ALL: [*Loud*]. *Ise-aaa!*

ONUOHA: [*In accord with tradition, presents the kola nuts to the King*]. *Oji Eze di Eze na aka.*

Ezeilo fishes out a large piece and bites it. Then the elders take their turns. The ceremonial cake went round in the hands of the elders like a ball in an electrified circle. Though no one spoke, yet the mastication sounds louder than cracked voices.

The kola nuts no doubt curse the tree that produced them and wish to escape from the oral cavities of the elders and King. But they are helpless just like games captured in a dragnet.

ONUOHA: We thank you for offering us kola nuts, our symbol of peace. And those who offer and accept peace shall find what?

CHIEFS: Peace.

ONUOHA: Yes. *Igwe*, [*Venerates*] we have come to apologize for what happened here last time. Men cease to make mistakes only when they are in the grave. When there is no mistake, there will be no correction and when there is no offence, there will be no forgiveness. So we are sorry and ask for your forgiveness.

EZEILO: [*Looks at each of them as they make remorseful gestures*]. Well, to err is human and forgiveness, divine. I have forgiven all of you present today. [*Sits up*]. But let me warn you all, I will not tolerate such disrespect from any of you again. Let such insolence never repeat itself.

UDOKASI: It won't.

EZEILO: [*Forces out a smile*]. It's okay. You are all welcomed.

ELUWA: [*Showers panegyric*]. Who says we have not a tolerant and understanding King. The gods bear witness today.

AKUBUIKE: That's correct! Absolutely correct Eluwa. [*Shake hands*].

ONUOHA: On behalf of the elders of our land, I am saying thank you for granting our request and may this brotherly love continue in this palace and in the land of Umuezeka.

To crown the reunion and put one and all on a merry mood, the King orders for palm wine. This sets a fire of jollification.

Elders bring out their cow-horns from their bags and helped themselves. *Ichie* Udokasi and *Nze* Akubuike are most ravished as they drank with fervor, rendering a medley of true and misleading encomium. The Bodyguards have no choice but to stand motionless and send back surging saliva down their esophagus.

As the Chiefs relish, a group of women and children enter the palace. The children cry for their fathers while the women weep for their husbands. *Ichie* Onuoha on behalf of the King stands and enquires from the peaceful demonstrators what has gone amiss.

SPOKESWOMAN: [*Face down in tears*]. O King, live forever. We are the wives and children of the Warriors of Umuezeka. Our husbands and fathers went out together yesterday and till today they have not returned. They have never gone out and not returned same day without notifying us. So we cry not knowing what has befallen them.

Children wail.

ONUOHA: It's all right. It's okay. Stop crying. The King is here; allow him   speak.

EZEILO: [*Stands*]. Our beloved wives and children, you said you haven't seen your husbands and fathers since yesterday?

DEMONSTRATORS: [*Chorus*]. Yes.

EZEILO: Didn't they tell you where they were going?

ALL: No.

EZEILO: Well, we wouldn't know either. However, don't cry as if you have confirmed them dead. As you know, they are able-bodied men who can take care of themselves, anywhere, anytime. It might be that they went for a big game and will come back sooner or later. So don't cry, but hopefully wait for their return. The bedbugs always wait for the hot water to get cold. So go back to your respective houses and still give them time to come back. Is that okay?

SPOKESWOMAN: [*Looks at her fellow women and they reluctantly nod their heads*]. Okay.

They walk out sluggishly but no longer crying aloud. The elders reason among themselves the sad news. As they discuss the issue, a distress voice is heard approaching. It is Atinga. He runs inside, shouting and panting. He falls in front of Ezeilo with his hands stretched out to his feet.

ATINGA: We are finished your Highness.

EZEILO: [*Kicks his hands away*]. Leave my feet before I finish you.

Bodyguards want to intervene, but the King stops them with a wave of hand. Atinga stands, shuddering.

AKUBUIKE: [*Semi-sozzled*]. Are you sure you are not half drunk? Because as much as I know, we haven't finished. Oh I see!

Your palm wine is finished. Come and
have some.

EZEILO: [*Intervenes*]. Let's listen to what he
has to say. [*To Atinga*]. You   better
compose yourself and speak sense else
you will get it hot. I won't entertain any
joke of yours.

ATINGA: King, as I was passing by the shrine-

.**ONONANKUME:** Which shrine?

ATINGA: The King's shrine, to empty the
refuse bin.

EZEILO: What happened? Did it scare you
that you emptied the refuse in front of
the shrine and ran here like a child who
saw a ghost?

ATINGA: [*Shakes his head*]. No, your
Highness.

EZEILO: [*Furiously*]. Then what happened?

ATINGA: [*Hesitates*]. The statue

EZEILO: The statue did what?

ATINGA: Is not there.

EZEILO: The huge image on the ironstone?

ATINGA: Yes your Highness.

EZEILO: You must be blind and crazy.

Ezeilo stands youthfully, shoves Atinga aside and trots to the shrine, while the Chiefs who still have their sense of reasoning and comprehension intact watch in bewilderment. When Ezeilo reached his shrine, he could not believe his eyes. He couldn't just believe that *arusi-odum*, he saw yesterday is no longer there. In a jiff, his world revolved. He sees a small bag on *odum's* stone, unties it and finds counterfeit cowries.

EZEILO: [*Stands enervated and frustrated*]. Does this mean these boys did this? This is incredible.

He contemplates meeting the killers to sort out the presumed issue, but unfortunately, he doesn't know their abode. He met them on the way as he returned from the Kings inter-town meeting in Umuasiama, native land of his mother in-law. Being highly frustrated, he gives up thinking.

EZEILO: I swear by the gods of my fathers, if they really did this, they shall pay with their lives.

Ezeilo walks angrily to the palace. As he enters, he looks at the Bodyguards with intrinsic indignation before sitting on his throne. The Guards were afraid at first but later took it to be one of his usual idiosyncrasies.

UDOKASI: What did you see your Highness?

ONONANKUME: Why do you ask? Our gods are never missing.

ONUOHA: Enough. Let us hear from the King.

EZEILO: [*Lifelessly*]. *Arusi-odum* has disappeared.

ALL: [*Shocked*]. Eh?

Bodyguards shudder. Some of the elders, who were semi-drunk, started coming back to their senses.

ONUOHA: [*Curious*]. Do you mean it was stolen?

EZEILO: [*Slowly*]. That is what I can't tell, but I did not see *Odum* in his tent. [*Pain and anger inundate his voice*].

CHIEFS: *Aru!*

AKUBUIKE: We are indeed finished.

Olachi enters quickly as she hears the sudden outcry of impending disaster. She goggles on seeing her Eze down in the dumps.

OLACHI: [*Anxiously*]. What is the problem, elders of our land? [*No response*].

Olachi stands motionless looking at her gloomy Ezeilo.

ONUOHA: [*Finds his tongue*]. Never has this happened in our land. Which callous men must have done this? [*Shakes his head sorrowfully*].

ELUWA: Oh! We are doomed.

OLACHI: [*Provoked by their words of bad omen*]. Why can't someone tell me what is going on here? Is someone dead?

In order to at least maintain the recent synergy, the elders did not speak of the grave and monumental consequences of *arusi-odum's* disappearance. Rather they tacitly decided to leave.

EZEILO: [*Sorrowfully*]. Are you leaving this all alone to me?

ONUOHA: [*Stammers*]. No, we shall be back. [*They left*].

Immediately Ezeilo accosts the Bodyguards with a fiery burning countenance.

EZEILO: Why did you betray me?

BODYGUARDS: [*Draws back in fear*]. Betray you?

EZEILO: [*Moving closer to them with great vexation*]. Why did you change the cowries to fake ones?

BODYGUARDS: [*Looks at each other*]. Fake?

EZEILO: [*Moving closer with vexation*]. Why didn't you give the men the cowries I gave you?

BODYGUARDS: [*Still moving retro as Ezeilo approaches angrily*]. We did.

EZEILO: Don't lie to me before I descend on you idiots.

Realizing, the wild fire in his eyes, they kneel down pleading for forgiveness; indirectly divulging their dishonest behaviour. Ezeilo is astonished and his temper triples.

Olachi who is yet to know the theme of the unfolding drama, wanted to stand in between to rescue the scare-stiff Bodyguards. She however draws back on perceiving the throbbing anger and agonizing disappointment in Ezeilo's face. In utter perplexity and fear, she stands aside gazing.

EZEILO: So you really did this to me. I trusted you, but you betrayed me – you senseless scorpions. [*Pronounces*]. Now, both of you will dance to the drumbeats of death.

Olachi understanding what this means, kneels begging for forgiveness on their behalf. The Queen and the Bodyguards pleaded and pleaded with tears but Ezeilo belligerent willpower neither yielded nor relinquished its vehemence.

Ezeilo sends for the Town Crier and orders him to announce to the whole town that Isiagboncha and Otikpo are responsible for the sudden disappearance of *arusi-odum*.

Immediately, townspeople converged at the palace. Out of rage and in honour of the King's word, which is unquestionable; the youths in a mob action overpowered the Bodyguards. They beat them severely and as custom demands, took them to the evil forest where they were beheaded with their own machetes.

ACT THREE

SCENE 1

That night was horrible for the people of Umuezeka. Ezeilo woke up before the first rooster crow and sat on his throne besieged with paralyzing thoughts. Some minutes later, Olachi joins him.

She is yet to fathom the gist of yesterday saga, which culminated in the gruesome execution of the two young men who have guarded his husband for a decade. After some minutes of pensive quietness, which Olachi decided to maintain knowing fully well who her husband is; Ezeilo on his own accord, brakes the ice.

EZEILO: Olachi, we have to leave this town today.

OLACHI [*Amazed*]. Eh? What? What did I hear you just say?

EZEILO: There is no water in my mouth. You heard me right. We are leaving Umuezeka for good.

OLACHI: You mean; you the *Igwe*, I the *Lolo* and Ikenga the Prince and heir to the throne will run away from Umuezeka?

EZEILO: Yes, if that is how you choose to put it.

OLACHI: [*Anxious*]. Why? For what? For who? Why must we leave our home? Our town! Our Kingdom! If there is something you are not telling me, please tell me. I don't understand you any longer. [*Sobbing*]. What is it Ezem? What is it that has made you lose prowess, to abandon the people under your care and leadership? What will make a hen leave her chicks? What -?

EZEILO: [*Interrupts impatiently*]. Enough woman! These emotionally laden questions of yours will lead us nowhere. The earlier we leave here the better for us.

OLACHI: [*Wipes her tears and gets up angrily*]. Enough, enough, that is what I have been getting lately. You no longer confide in me as your wife, neither do you tell me what happens in the town nor in this palace. You no longer behave like Ezem I used to admire for his bravery and fearlessness even in the face of death. Look, I am not moving an inch unless I know what has made a man decide to leave his roof, royalty for crying out loud sake.

EZEILO: Very well then. You can stay here and bury your dead. As for me I am leaving this land tonight with my son. [*About to enter inside*].

OLACHI: [*Holds Ezeilo, kneeling*]. Please don't do this to me. How can I leave without you and my only child? How can a child grow properly without the mother? Please don't leave me empty handed.

EZEILO: [*Raises her slowly and passionately to her feet*]. You are getting the whole thing wrong. Listen to me. The more we stay here, the nearer we approach death. [*Olachi raise eyebrows*]. An unprecedented terrible thing has happened in Umuezeka. [*Emphatic*]. *Arusi-odum* is missing. And according to tradition, royal sacrifice is required to appease the gods. Though I won't be sacrificed, I don't want my son to be sacrificed either.

OLACHI: [*Gasp in panic*]. I will. I will do as you say.

The Queen goes inside and hurriedly prepares for their departure. Ezeilo wish mother earth would open her mouth and swallow him. How on earth will he live happily for this cowardly act he is embarking on? But he doesn't want his son dead. The devil and the deep blue sea; he has to choose one.

EZEILO: [*To himself*]. Why has all my plans and actions to save my only son turned to naught? My trusted Bodyguards betrayed me, who then can I trust? [*Shakes his head*]. Here is no longer safe for me and my family. I better be a father than a King who has no heir.

OLACHI: [*Enters with Ikenga tied on her back, carrying her luggage and her son's box*]. I am set my lord.

EZEILO: Come and sit.

OLACHI: The child will be uncomfortable.

Ezeilo walks to her and place his right arm across her shoulders. Olachi catches her breath audibly.

EZEILO: No, no, don't cry my love. It will be alright. It is just a matter of time, okay. [*Olachi nods in sobs*]. I assure you. [*Calls*]. Atinga.

The happy-go-lucky servant enters.

ATINGA: [*Prostrate*]. Yes your Highness.
EZEILO: Go and get ready, you will accompany *Lolo*.
ATINGA: To where?
EZEILO: Don't be silly boy. Just go and get ready for the journey.
ATINGA: [*Bows*]. Yes your Highness [*Enters inside*].
OLACHI: [*Cleaning her tears*]. Where are we going?
EZEILO: Utogidi
OLACHI: My father's house?
EZEILO: Yes.
OLACHI: We will live there?

EZEILO: No. I will join you there tonight, after putting certain things in order. Then tomorrow we will head to Mbasa, my mother's place.

OLACHI: [*Tenderly*]. Ezem.

EZEILO: Yes.

OLACHI: Promise me, you will surely come tonight.

EZEILO: How can I abandon my wife and my only son? It is only a fool that will leave his yams in another man's barn. [*Cocksure*]. I promise and have never failed.

ATINGA: [*Shoddily enters*]. Your Highness, I am ready.

EZEILO: Okay. Follow the Queen, while she leads the way.

ATINGA: [*Slaphappy*]. No problem, your Highness. I will guide from the back.

Olachi gives him a disgusting look.

EZEILO: [*To Olachi*]. Please take good care of him. [*Caresses Ikenga*]. May the gods protect you. Safe journey. [*Ere they went out of sight, Ezeilo calls and Olachi halts.*

He walks to her]. Ike-nna-ya. Ikenga, my son. [*Caresses his tender cheeks once more. Removes one of his royal ornaments and puts it on his neck*]. This is yours from now onwards. [*He kisses Olachi and Ikenga, and bids them farewell*].

The daredevil is already on his way to unknown destination. Olachi walks down the path reluctantly. She halts and catches a glimpse of her husband's shadowy posterior, then exit.

SCENE 2

Members of the *Igwe*'s cabinet are seated at Onuoha's compound. They are about to commence an extra-ordinary meeting, without the knowledge of the King. Sadness owing to the recent taboo and its colossal consequence is clearly seen in their cloudy faces and agitated postures.

The Prime Minister, *Ichie* Onuoha stands and set the ball rolling with a parabolic oration, which freed the discomfited elders from a hovering doom that flung them into the cesspit of fear.

ONUOHA: [*Shredding the repellent silence*]. Elders of our great land, I greet you all. [*They reciprocate*]. Why are we folding our arms and sitting like women? Men are known for action. The hen does not remain calm when one tampers with her eggs neither does she fold her hands and watch the kite snatch her chick without a fight.

UDOKASI: [*Chips in*]. You are right *Ichie* Onuoha.

ONUOHA: So we should not be weak but strong and do what is expected of us and at the right time too. Procrastination is precarious [*Sits*].

UDOKASI: Thank you *Ichie* Onuoha. You have spoken well. That is why I always say our land is blessed not only with material wealth but also with wise men. Let me tell you fellow elders of

Umuezeka, though a duck walks on land, it flies when the kite snatches her duckling. [*Sits abruptly*].

AKUBUIKE: [*Stands*]. Yes. We shouldn't act like cowardly hirelings that take to their heels at the sight of a wolf coming to destroy their flock. And the earlier we become bold to face the wolf, the better for us and our people. I greet you all.

OKWUDIRI: [*Enters hastily*]. I greet you all. [*Silence responds*].

ONONANKUME: [Stands energetically]. It appears you all are beating about the bush and afraid to hit the nail on the head. My father when he was alive, use to say that it is only a foolhardy favour-seeker that will sit on the fence and not hit the nail of truth on the head of lie, when he or she is inside the den of destruction. And I hold that, it is only a mentally ill person that sleeps when his house is on fire.

Elders of our land, it is not doing the things that we like, but liking to do the things that we have to do, that makes life worthwhile. With due respect, since our King, His Royal Highness Ezeilo has failed in his primary duty of safeguarding *arusi-odum*, the god of war and life, tradition should prevail!

OKWUDIRI: What tradition, if I may ask?

ONONANKUME: You may not ask. So keep quiet, latecomer.

OKWUDIRI: Me, latecomer.

ONONANKUME: Yes, you. Or is it a lie? And if it is true, why won't I say it?

OKWUDIRI: [*Retaliates*]. Well, I don't misuse my precious strength talking to whippersnappers.

ONONANKUME: What? [*Ticked off*]. You call me a fool? [*Moves closer to Okwudiri*]. You think I don't know?

A brawl ensues. They duel with their third legs. *Ichie* Udokasi and *Nze* Eluwa intervene.

ONONANKUME: [*Still peeved*]. I don't blame you. If not for my kind-hearted father who paid your father's debt, you wouldn't have been here, not to talk of speaking so rudely and foolishly to me.

You would have been sold as a slave to the wicked white men and would be washing plates or clothes for them now.

OKWUDIRI: [*Chafed*]. Don't provoke me. [*Pause*]. But wait; did I hear you say wicked whites?

UDOKASI: Enough of these talks. We are elders, and elders of our land are known for discipline and integrity.

OKWUDIRI: Thank you very much, *Ichie* Udokasi. I know you are peace loving. But for the sake of fair-hearing allow him answer my simple question.

ONONANKUME: Yes, I said so and what about that?

OKWUDIRI: Well they may be wicked, but not as heartless as those who stole *arusi*. Isn't it better to be a slave there, than to be a freeborn here and be deprived the basic right of freedom of speech? And if I were there washing plates, perhaps after some years, I would be richer than you and Akugburugburu, the wealthiest man in our community. And you know what, whenever I return, you all will bow for me. Now tell me, did your father do me good or bad?

ONONANKUME: It is people like you that are of little or no worth to their homeland. As long as you prefer another man's own to yours, you will never move forward.

ONUOHA: It is enough. We did not come here to quarrel or exchange words like teenagers or market women, but for a crucial purpose.

OKWUDIRI: What is it, if I may ask? [*To Onuoha*].

ONONANKUME: You see. He has started again.

ONUOHA: [*To Ononankume*]. Never mind. [*To Okwudiri*]. What I am saying is that we are here to discuss an issue so important like life and death. There are many other matters but this one is very important.

His speech though porous and superficial, seems to have poured oil on trouble waters. As they are about to progress, a man stumbles in. His outfit portrays one who has run amok. He is wearing a dirty singlet on a worn out blue short sleeves shirt. Below his trunk, is a form-fitting jump-up trouser that has two large eyes at the butt.

On his feet, is an unpaired slippers. On his wrist is a chronometer that has neither ticked for a long time nor intends to do so in the near future. Yet he feels high and important. His hair is unkempt. His beard ragged. His oral cavity stinks of rotgut. Nonetheless he speaks unrestrainedly, puking nonsense sense.

Whereas some elders know him in person, others know him only by name. The bottle of palm wine in his back pocket coupled with his stomach, which is temporarily impregnated by alcohol; readily suggests that he is most likely a retired palm wine taper, receiving his pension from liquor – a renowned and experienced drunkard.

OKWUDIRI: Akpuruka, you have come to disturb us. We are not in the mood to entertain any form of distraction. So leave, if you don't mind.

AKPURUKA: [*Stoned*]. Why won't I mind? Don't you have mind? What kind of oral

English is that? Anyway, you are just a fusspot and not wine pot, so I will forgive you when you commit grammatical *bladder*.

For your information, it is only troublemakers that disturb. As for respectable retired but not tired drinkers like me, I herald glad tidings of peace and security, and stand by it as long as palm wine trees stand in the farms and forests.

ONUOHA: [*Scornfully*]. Yes, you are right.

AKPURUKA: Why not, if not. He, who drinks white wine, never tells black lies. For I am a man of honour; executing the bidding of the gods.

ONUOHA: [*Irate*]. Fine. But leave us; we are having a crucial meeting.

AKPURUKA: How *cruising* is it? [*Demonstrates*]. More than that I do with my bottles? To hell with it. [*Tapping his chest*]. I, Highly Respected, Warrior, Father, Grandfather, Native Doctor, Chief Akpuruka, is superior to your meeting. Do all of you put together, drink as much as I do? Or do you see what I see thereafter? [*Speaks to himself, snickering*]. How shall they see, when they don't wash their eyes with white wine?

ONONANKUME: [*Ireful*]. Afo-nkwu.

AKPURUKA: That's my nickname.

ONONANKUME: [*Shouts*]. Akpuruka.

AKPURUKA: This is the real one.

ONONANKUME: [*Pointing at him with his index finger*]. You are disturbing the peace of this meeting. It is high time you leave.

AKPURUKA: [*Sharply*]. I won't leave till it is low time. In fact I will not leave unless you bless me. [*Staggers and sits on the ground*]. You amateur drunkards are here chanting peace in pieces while some are running to true peace, the land of promise, paradise coming down from palm wine trees. Even the *Lolo* has finished the race, and awaits her crown.

ONUOHA: [*Ears twitch*]. What do you mean by that? Is it a new parable or is it the wine playing its remarkable role?

AKPURUKA: Thanks a million to palm wine. Who knows what life would have been without it? That is why you all did not see or perceived what I did this morning and will never. For where there is no palm wine, there is no foresight and the people perish.

ONUOHA: [*Repugnantly*]. What is it that you saw, that we who are much older and experienced haven't seen?

AKPURUKA: Top secret, concealed in my stomach. And unless you please my stomach, it will padlock my mouth.

ELUWA: [*Aggressive*]. Can't you see he is drunk? He only wants wine. [*To Onuoha*].

AKPURUKA: I am happy you know that. One bottle of palm wine – no less, no more. [*Slaps his palms on the muddy floor*].

ONUOHA: [*Tricky*]. Okay, I will give you.

Akpuruka smiles clumsily.

ONUOHA: But first, you will tell us the secret.

AKPURUKA: No. Stomach will be angry for my mouth, if it receives not the wine first.

ONUOHA: On the contrary, it cannot be angry for the mouth that feeds it.

AKPURUKA: [*Stands and staggers*]. Very well, I will reveal the secret but remember you promise to give me a bottle of wine, no less, no more. Remember you are an honourable man and an elder. The gods of palm trees won't be happy with you if you promise and fail. You have given your word to give me my wine. [*Onuoha nods. Akpuruka brings out the empty bottle in his rear pocket*]. You see this bottle?

ONUOHA: [*Contemplating*]. Yes. What is it for?

AKPURUKA: [*With an aura of importance*]. It signifies the significance of palm wine. [*Staggers close to Onuoha*].

ONONANKUME: What is all this melodrama for? We have an important issue to tackle. Can't you see he is simply intoxicated? [*Speaking to Ichie Onuoha*].

AKPURUKA: [*To Onuoha*]. Don't mind him. He was drinking all night with Mazi Okwudiri.

OKWUDIRI: [*Angrily*]. Enough of that insolence, you wine bag.

AKPURUKA: Wine bag, agreed. Even palm bag accepted.

AKUBUIKE: [*Frustrated*]. Where emanated this hopeless obstacle of a drunk. Look at how his breath reeks of alcohol.

AKPURUKA: Better to emit liquor than utter lies. Moreover I don't shovel snuff into my nose like you. I only drink and it is not a sin. Even the Holy Book as I learnt says; take a little wine for thy stomach sake. Or is it because, most of you have refused to accept the gospel? Let me tell you even though I am an obstacle, yet I am not hopeless. I am hopeful that one day the people of Umuezeka would be converted by the ghost man, sorry the white man. And will join me to become practicing Christians.

ONONANKUME: Our ancestors forbid. You alone will be his adherent.

AKPURUKA: No problem. Time will tell.

AKUBUIKE: If I may ask you drunkard of a Christian. What you are consuming, is it little wine?

AKPURUKA: Well, it depends on what you mean by little. What may be little to you may be nothing to me. And what may be little to me may be big for you, depending on a lot of factors like; the size of your stomach, propensity to consume, number of years of experience you have in active alcoholic service etc. [*Tries to obfuscate*]. You see even Rabbi appreciated the importance of wine that is why his first miracle was turning water into wine.

OKWUDIRI: Come, when did you start attending the white man's church service that you seem to know much about his religion?

AKPURUKA: You see, as a talented town crier, I don't need to attend his service, at least not regularly, before I know what he and his group teach. Neither do I intend to reveal my uncountable confidential sources of information. [*To Onuoha*]. Come my dear friend. [*Stretch out his hand*]. Hold this bottle and promise it wine. Sorry for the interruption, first of all.

Akpuruka seems to be presiding over the meeting as a result of the apparent compromising posture of Onuoha. This displeases his colleagues. However they hold their peace. After Onuoha's promise, Akpuruka let the cat out the bag.

AKPURUKA: For the first time in my life, I saw our beautiful *Lolo* walking down the border bush path early this morning with her belongings including some bottles of foreign wine.

ONUOHA: Now I perceive that you not only inebriated but also mentally deranged.

AKPURUKA: [*Beckoning with his fingers*]. Descend more grammars.

ONUOHA: You have overstayed your welcome, so move out. [*Authoritative*].

AKPURUKA: [*Ignoring him*]. The child was also tied on her back. [*Elders look at each other*]. Oh! How I wish I had the chance to say farewell with a bottle of palm wine. [*Sighs*].

ONUOHA: [*Disturbed*]. Look Akpuruka, if this is a pre-meditated ruse for wine, I am sorry you won't get it. So you can go with your silly report.

AKPURUKA: I have said the truth and nothing but a drunkard's truth. So let me have my bottle of wine, no less, no more. No breaching of wine contract. Its consequences are disastrous. [*Loll*].

Looking at each other, the elders *sotto voce* consider the potential of truth in Akpuruka's statement. As they discuss with their eyes, heads and hands; Akpuruka to some extent cease to be a dimwitted blighter. In other not to take chances, they resolved to visit the palace straight away.

Okwudiri is directed to get some male youths in case Akpuruka's story is true. The elders march to the palace.

AKPURUKA: [*Gabbles*]. Where are you all emigrating to? [*Elders out of sight*]. Wait. Wait. My stomach is angry for you drunkards. And if not appeased, Umuezeka will know no peace. I hope you heard that? Of course, you did. You all are not deaf, at least, not at the same time. Wait! Wait!! I say, wait. [*Follows them woozily*].

SCENE 3

On getting to the King's palace, the Chiefs notice upheavals. Baggage and valuable property are kept in rows as if to be auctioned. Also, the palace is extraordinarily quiet. However, to avoid jumping into hasty conclusion, they employ facial tranquility to conceal their disturbed and suspicious state of mind.

King Ezeilo inevitably welcomes them with suppressed panic. He feigns to be at ease, ever ready, strong as an ox and bold as a lion. Attributes he has impressed in the psyche of his people. To further attenuate suspicion, he lingers a smile on his naturally mean face. This made him look more like one who is frowning than smiling. The Chiefs reciprocate. Yet vehement skepticism fills their hearts.

ONUOHA: [*Considers Ezeilo's smile which is turning to a grin, as first in   annals*].
O King may you live long. [*Prostates and others did same*].
EZEILO: [*Serpentine smile*]. Thank you, my Chiefs. May you also live long.

ALL: Isee-eeh!

ONUOHA: [*Looks suspiciously at Ezeilo and clears his throat loudly*]. Our people hold that when an elder starts a speech by clearing his throat then he is about to say something hard or uncommon to the ears. Again, our people say that the toad does not run in the daytime for naught. Either something is after it or it is after something.

AKPURUKA: [*Stumbles in*]. Exactly! I am after my wine. [*Though stupefied by the liquid demon, Akpuruka was still able to differentiate royalty from commoner. He prostrates with his buttocks protruded skywards*]. O King li, live forever!

EZEILO: Yes my son. How are you today?

AKPURUKA: Always agile. [*Rubbing his stomach*]. As long as my warehouse is not empty.

Ezeilo immediately understand what Akpuruka wants. He excused himself and went inside. The Chiefs also comprehend what Akpuruka is indirectly requesting. But what they can't figure out is why the King should do the errand of getting the wine himself? Where are his servants? What of Atinga? Does this authenticate the drunkard's bulletin? They pondered over this, whispering to each other. Nonetheless, they agreed to still hold their peace and allow the water boil to hundred degrees centigrade before bringing down the kettle.

Being catapulted into an elated trance by the expectation of palm wine, Akpuruka disrupts the present silence of the palace with a poetic eulogy. This panegyric he either composed on the spur of the moment or retrieved from his cranial archive and rendered it like a rhymester.

AKPURUKA: O! How precious is wine
    The only pure water in this dirty world
    White as snow
    Pure as *eligwe*

    By it, palm trees are proud
    Kegs, cow horns, bellies are filled
    Soils fertilized
    Leaving our stomachs cleansed

With it warriors defeat their
opponents
Captives set free
Kings come and go
Leaving royal heritage to their
heirs

But the taper taps always
Topers on their frequencies
Ancestors receive their fair share
Making us visionary messengers

As the Chiefs watch and listen to him with an ambivalent sense of admiration and pity, King Ezeilo comes out with two jars of palm wine. This threw Akpuruka into a manic state of ecstasy.

EZEILO: Akpuruka

AKPURUKA: [*Bows*]. Yes, your Highest Highness!

EZEILO: This is all yours. [*Hands him a jar, smiling*].

AKPURUKA: Ha! [*Collects and prostate*]. *Igwe-eee!* May you live forever wine! May those who seek this throne get it only on their sick beds. [*Ezeilo nods*]. And let all those who seek your life stay alive with leprosy.

EZEILO: [*With some others*]. Isea!

AKPURUKA: I am just being magnanimous; if not, I would say let them die outright. [*On his feet*]. For anointing me with [*raises the jar of palm wine*] this special oil this bright day, you are now my special friend, as long as the status quo is maintained.

EZEILO: That's no problem.

AKPURUKA: Ha! Then you have no problem. Just wait and see how I will proclaim your name and works to the uttermost part of the earth and skyrocket your throne.

Where is that town crier? I have said it time without number that that lazy town crier needs to be relieved of his job. Let me perform dual function for you. Don't worry, I will give him a little of this, [*raises the wine*] so that he can hammer, harp and even trumpet your acts of benevolence, generosity and good leadership. In fact I will do it myself. I will cry in the town like a baby. [*To himself*]. Who says we don't have a good King? A King who even accommodates drunkards like me? Unlike some who fail when they promise, you keep yours even when you have not promised.

Those who say you won't rule will either die before their last-born or like the enemies of UDU – Umuezeka Drinkers Union. Let them choose one. [*Ezeilo laughs*]. No, this is not a laughing matter. Such an act of charity in this time of utmost selfishness should be taken seriously and appreciated immensely. Look, those who say you and your sons would not sit on this throne will die untimely leaving their palm wine trees for me and my union members. [*Ezeilo chuckles*]. You just leave that to me and see how I will chase your enemies out of this town with the palm wine taper's knife.

EZEILO: [*Hails*]. Akpuruka.

AKPURUKA: Yes, that is my name, the only
but one name given to me but one   day.
[*Yawns uncivilly*].

EZEILO: The only son of the famous palm
wine taper.

AKPURUKA: You are not far from the truth.

EZEILO: Winebibber of repute; legacy from the
ancestors.

AKPURUKA: You are the King, no one else.
[Walks out *and chants*]. Today, today,
tomorrow no more, if I wine today, I will
dine no more.

Holding his tub of wine as if it is a
reliquary, Akpuruka makes a red-blooded exit,
systematically increasing and decreasing his
buttocks.

The elders are flabbergasted by the
eccentric behaviour of the King, wondering
when he started entertaining drunkards in his
palace. But perhaps he did what he did to
diffuse the envisaged purpose of the Chiefs
visit. Nonetheless, their suspense is sustained
and curiosity soar.

SCENE 4

King Ezeilo proffers palm wine to the Chiefs but they reject with a couth sense of purpose. They are suspicious of the unusual red carpet reception. Having exhausted their packs of patience, the Chiefs led by Onuoha cast the die.

ONUOHA: First of all, I salute you for your kind gesture, but as our people say, a man doesn't go picnicking while his roof is licking or sleeps when his house is on fire. We have come to hear from the horse's mouth whether what we are hearing is true or not.

EZEILO: [*Apply defense mechanism of aggression and impoliteness*]. What is it that has been disturbing your eardrums?

ONUOHA: Something unheard of. Any way, it is a rumour.

EZEILO: What rumour?

ONONANKUME: [*Interrupts diplomatically*]. *Igwe, Lolo* haven't come out to greet us neither have I heard the cry of her baby since we came. Aren't they inside?

EZEILO: [*Intrinsic panic*]. My wife is sleeping and must the boy cry always? [*Camouflage calmness*]. Both are sleeping. Is that okay?

The Chiefs glance at each other. Some wish Akpuruka had not left, so that they would teach him the demerits of being a drunk who derives pleasure in manufacturing pranks that taints the King's image. Some however are not satisfied with the King's reply, and were about to ask of Atinga before Okwudiri and his armies storm the palace.

EZEILO: [*Infuriated but inwardly afraid*]. What business do you have here? [*To Okwudiri*]. And who are these rascals?

Without answering and consulting his fellow elders he winks at the able-bodied youths and they desecrate the sacred floors in search of the Queen and Prince.

Ezeilo protests madly, but the youth had their way. Undoubtedly, the eternal absence of

Isiagboncha and Otikpo facilitated their prowess and success.

The Chiefs are mystified but allow things to sort out themselves. The boys come out later and announce their findings to the Chiefs' astonishment.

ONUOHA: [*Alarmed*]. It can't be true.

Still finding it incredible, the Chiefs, except *Nze* Okwudiri, enter to see things for themselves.

Ezeilo not knowing what to do wants to scamper but is halted by the youths at the command of Okwudiri. At this point, Ezeilo wish that the ground tear asunder and swallow him than to face the music chiefly orchestrated by his archenemy.

Inside, the Chiefs holler one abomination of desolation after another, only to come out and be dumfounded.

OKWUDIRI: I believed it. I know that drunkards like Akpuruka, don't lie like that especially when they are drunk.

ONUOHA: [*Recovering from the shock*]. May the gods of Umuezeka forbid! [*Bitter, but speaks to the King with respect*]. *Igwe*, so you were planning to run away?

Ezeilo keeps quiet.

ONUOHA: *Igwe* Ezeilo, where is your son? Where have you taken him to?

Ezeilo remains silent. This arouses Onuoha's anger.

ONUOHA: Do you want us to die for your shortcoming? Do you want us all to be visited by the wrath of *odum* through drought, pestilence and invasion of our land? Is it your wish that the people of famous Umuezeka die without remnants? Is that what you want? Tell me.

EZEILO: [*Fumes*]. Neither is my innocent child a better substitute. [*Bravely*]. Take me instead.

ONUOHA: That is uncalled for and unheard of. A man and a leader for that matter should be ready to face the consequences of his actions and inactions.

You are saddled with the responsibility of safeguarding *arusi-odum* as the King. You failed in this regard. And as tradition demands, you are to sacrifice your child for your pitfall, so as to appease the gods and ward off their pernicious anger. The reason for this is to make Kings take the safeguard of *arusi-odum,* god of life, war and protection, serious.

Rather, you sneaked him away probably together with *Lolo* and Atinga, who are nowhere to be found also. Do you want us to die? Do you want thousands to perish for one child? [*Sternly*]. Now, where did you send them?

Ezeilo utters no word.

OKWUDIRI: [*Vituperates cheekily*]. Where is the cursed child, you weakling of a King?

EZEILO: [*Looks horrifically at Okwudiri*]. How
    dare you abuse me?

ONONANKUME: That is insignificant when
    compared to your abominable abuse of
    the people and gods of our land.

ONUOHA: For the last time, where did you
    send the boy?

EZEILO: I rather die than tell you.

When the Chiefs perceive that Ezeilo
was unyielding, they were frustrated. Vexed in
unison, they agreed to incarcerate him, till he
reveals his son's where about. Consequently,
he was disrobed of his royal garb and put in
prison by the youths at the order of *Ichie*
Onuoha. The men also took back his luggage.

For security reasons, two men are
stationed at the entrance of the prison.
Another four kept watch and ward over the
palace on two men per week shift basis. Tired
and still surprised, the Chiefs exit in despair
and dismal, swinging their heads to the east
and west.

Due to the way things fell apart, Ezeilo
is vehemently bitter. He is particularly upset

because of Okwudiri's antagonistic insults and worried about his wife and son.

ACT FOUR

SCENE 1

Twenty-four years later, the wanted baby has become a full-grown man. He is veritably endowed with burly biceps and stamina. He lives with his mother, Olachi and Ifeuwabunike, his mother's uncle but whom he knows as his father.

Atinga returned to his father's house, twenty-two years ago. That was when Olachi was driven away from her father's house by his brother, Ashimeleze – the first son of their late father.

On arrival, Olachi told his brother why they came on exile and that Ezeilo will come later in the day to explain more. The day turned into days, days to weeks, weeks into months and months to years. Thinking that Olachi has done something abominable and was just deceiving him, he sent her packing. So she took refuge in her uncle's house.

Olachi is now gaunt, not due to malnourishment or age as it were. But she is distressed owing to the perennial absence of her husband. If he is dead or alive, she knows not.

Ikenga comes out with a hoe on his beefy shoulders.

IKENGA: What is it mother? You look worried. [*Takes a close look at his agonized mother*].

OLACHI: [*Feigns cheer*]. Nothing my son, I am fine.

IKENGA: Sure?

OLACHI: [*Smiles*]. I am okay. By the way, have you taken your breakfast?

IKENGA: Yes. Thanks for the delicious food.

OLACHI: Thank God my son.

IKENGA: Let me go and help father in the farm.

OLACHI: Alright. Take care.

Ikenga exit.

OLACHI: God, please preserve this only seed of solace for me. [*Solemnly*].

After sunset, Olachi sits cracking palm kernels. Suddenly she pauses and gaze in self-hypnotism, looking at nothing in particular. Ezeilo has become an impalpable figure lurking in her mind. Ifeuwabunike walks in without her noticing.

IFEUWABUNIKE: [*Drops his machete and hoe*]. What is it again, Ola? I have told you time without number to stop worrying yourself. If you continue this way, you might die before your time. [*Sits beside her*]. Look, I suppose by now it is obvious that Ezeilo is dead and the earlier you realize and accept it, the better for you.

OLACHI: [*Sharply*]. No, he isn't dead. My Eze is not dead. [*Sobs*].

IFEUWABUNIKE: Sorry. But you see he can't be alive all these years without looking for you. At least if not for anything for his son, his first son, the first fruit of his lions. [*Olachi sobs more and more. He holds her shoulders gently and consoles her*]. Look at me. [*Olachi wipes her tears with her palm*]. I am your uncle and will

not do anything to hurt your feelings,
but you have to face reality. Life is all
about changes, constant ones for that
matter. The earlier you begin to adapt to
the inevitable vagaries of life, the
happier you become.

OLACHI: Happiness? How does a woman feel
happy without her husband? Without
seeing him dead or alive for twenty four
good years? Tell me, how? [*Starts
crying*].

IFEUWABUNIKE: [*Consoles her*]. I really
understand how you feel. [*Softly*]. Same
way I felt twenty-five years ago when
Adaugo left me with a stillbirth after
eight years of childless marriage.

OLACHI: And you don't still feel same way?

IFEUWABUNIKE: [*Inhale and exhale breath*].
Well, I do, but not as then. [*Enunciates*].
Truly real love never dies, knows no
bounds. [*Manly*]. But I advised you to
remarry, a year after your arrival.

OLACHI: It is easier said than done. [*Somber*].
No other man born of a woman can fill
the vacuum created by Ezeilo in my

heart. [*Turns to his uncle*]. If I may ask, why didn't you do same?

IFEUWABUNIKE: Really it is difficult, very hard to forget a loved one. But as a man, I can still at my age marry a girl young enough to be my daughter. It is not so with you women.

OLACHI: Then, let me be.

Ikenga returns from the farm exhausted.

IKENGA: [*Drops his hoe*]. What is the matter? You both look sad.

OLACHI: No, nothing my son. [*Cleans her tears with the edge of her wrapper*].

IFEUWABUNIKE: Welcome my son. Did you finish the clearing?

IKENGA: [*Proudly*]. I left no grass. The whole farmland is ready for planting.

IFEUWABUNIKE: That's good my son. For that you've got yourself two cowries.

IKENGA: [*Exhilarated*]. Thank you father.

IFEUWABUNIKE: Go inside my room, under the couch you will find a pouch. Take two cowries from it.

As Ikenga enters happily, Olachi calls.

IKENGA: Yes mother.

OLACHI: Go to the kitchen and take your food. It is inside the small mortar.

IKENGA: Okay mother. [*Enters gaily*].

OLACHI: Go in and have your lunch too, you must be hungry.

IFEUWABUNIKE: Yes. [*Peeps behind and whispers*]. Try and be yourself, okay?

Olachi nods and Ifeuwabunike enters.

IKENGA: [*Shouts from within, minutes later*]. Nne, won't you join us?

OLACHI: I will, just get the ball rolling.

Olachi hammers the palm kernels with renewed zest. After filling a plate, she joins them.

SCENE 2

At night after dinner, Ikenga sits close to his mother at the inglenook while Ifeuwabunike is asleep. Their somber silhouettes are seen extending to a lawn illuminated by moonlight.

IKENGA: Mother.

OLACHI: Yes.

IKENGA: Did father beat you?

OLACHI: [*Surprised*]. How can?

IKENGA: Did he speak rudely to you?

OLACHI: No. Why these questions?

IKENGA: When I came back from the farm today, you were shedding tears.

OLACHI: Well, that's wise of you. But what happened was that I ate some onion bulbs when preparing lunch and naturally it produces tears. Moreover, your father cannot do such a thing like that. He is a good man; caring, brave and responsible. I hope you would be like him?

IKENGA: More than him.

OLACHI: You believe so?

IKENGA: Yes.

OLACHI: May it be as you believe. After all, that is what it should be. A son should be greater than the father, just as a student should be better than the teacher. [Brief pause]. It is late. Go and sleep so that you will wake up early to help your father in the farm tomorrow.

IKENGA: [*Stands*]. Okay. Goodnight mother.

OLACHI: Goodnight Ikem. [*Looks at him with mixed feeling of admiration and fear, as he goes to bed. Admiration for his bravery and wisdom, fear that he may later find out the truth of his paternity*]. Protect him [*Looking upwards*] for me, I beg. [*Enter inside*].

Lately, fear of the unknown seems to have made Olachi to immensely adhere to the new religion.

SCENE 3

Olachi is in front of the hut, simultaneously cutting slices from a bunch of breadfruit with her right hand and pressing out the seeds with the thumb and index finger of her left.

Ikenga wakes up long after the third cockcrow. He comes out, yawning like a refugee. A cloth hung on his neck, dangling towards mother earth.

IKENGA: Good morning ma.

OLACHI: Good morning my son. You woke late.

IKENGA: It was the night talk.

OLACHI: That is why I usually tell you to sleep in time, but you like moonlight stories.

IKENGA: But that is the only time, I have fun. You know the village boys and girls don't associate with me.

OLACHI: Alright. [*Pause*]. Enhh, your father said you should meet him at the farm so as to help him plant the yams.

IKENGA: Okay, let me wash my face.

OLACHI: Before you go, take my sheep out for grazing.

IKENGA: Yes ma.

Ikenga goes inside, washes his face, and hurries out with the sheep. At the grassland, he meets two brothers and their flock grazing. He gives them ten yards, but they seem not contented.

CHIMAOBI: Are you blind? Can't you see our herds are grazing on this land? [*Shrewdly*].

IKENGA: But I have left that area for you.

NNAEMEKA: [*Belligerently*]. Are your deaf? Can't you hear the hungry bleating of our sheep?

IKENGA: [*Retorts*]. So are my sheep too.

NNAEMEKA: If you think you can leave your father's land and come to Utogidi to drag grassing land with us, you have made a very big mistake.

IKENGA: [*Embarrassed*]. And what is that supposed to mean?

CHIMAOBI: Go and ask your mother, you bastard stranger.

Together they mockingly laugh at Ikenga. He tried to bear it but when he could not, he furiously attacks them. Ikenga was physically and mentally enkindled. He fought like a superman, having an extra Y-chromosome aberration. Solely, he taught the duo the lesson of their lives. When he was about to feed one of them with sand, which is the traditional seal of defeat, they escaped narrowly leaving their famished bleating flock just as hirelings do at the sight of a wolf.

IKENGA: [*Shouting in triumph*]. Why are you running away? Come and graze your sheep in your father's land, greedy fools!

Without wasting much time, he takes the sheep home. Olachi was tiding the house. He pitches the sheep at their steads and goes to his mother.

OLACHI: So quick - ?
IKENGA: [*Stern*]. Mother.
OLACHI: Yes.
IKENGA: Who is my father?
OLACHI: [*Astound*]. What sort of question is that?
IKENGA: I am sorry mother. I only wanted to ascertain –

OLACHI: Ascertain what? Did anybody tell you that your father is no longer your father?

Opuruiche and her bruised sons, barge in. She tied her head-tie round her waist.

IKENGA: Look at them.

OLACHI: Who? What happened? [*Confused*].

OPURUICHE: *Ehhn*, there you are. Olachi, why did you send your son to kill my sons with your witchcraft? Am I the one who prevented you from having more than one?

IKENGA: [*Intervenes*]. Don't call my mother a witch again.

Olachi restrains him.

OPURUICHE: No! Why withhold him? Allow him. Or are you pretending not to be poisonous. Why not leave him to perpetuate your wicked devices that threw you out of your husband's house. For the last time, I warn you. Leave me and my children alone. There is no business between humans and witches and wizards.

As for you, [*beaming her satellite eyes on Ikenga*] the next time you touch my sons, I will make sure I send you back to where you belong. [*To her sons*]. Let's go.

They march out like guard of war. Opuruiche really dealt on a chapter in Olachi's life that hurts her deeply. Being in anguish, she could not utter a word.

Ikenga is surprised and filled with indignation for her mother's silence to such disparaging statements most especially about his paternity.

IKENGA: Mother.

OLACHI: [*Tensed*]. Ye-s.

IKENGA: Do not lie to me this time.

OLACHI: About what?

IKENGA: Who is my real father?

OLACHI: [*Stutter*]. What do you mean?

IKENGA: [*Mean*]. Answer my question mother.

Realizing that the cat has been let out of the bag, Olachi couldn't face her son. She could not afford telling him the truth, and couldn't lie either.

Being in dilemma, she seems to take momentary solace in silence. But Ikenga was too angry to bear it. He moves inside and comes out shortly with his luggage.

OLACHI: [*Frightened*]. Why are you carrying your bag?

IKENGA: I am going.

OLACHI: Going where?

IKENGA: [*Retorts*]. To my father's house of course! I can't bear these grave unexplained insults and feeling of being unwanted anymore. [*Dawns on him*]. No wonder, they don't socialize with me. Mother, you have deceived me for long. Goodbye. [*Runs away*].

Olachi runs after him, pleading and promising to tell him the whole truth, all to no avail. He was infuriated for being deceived for so long by his mother he loved so much.

Indeed sometimes, we love to a climax and hatred, that is as strong as the love, creeps in.

Ikenga runs away faster in anger and sorrow, not knowing where he runs to. Olachi returns, not being able to meet his pace.

After some time, Ifeuwabunike returns from the farm, tired. He is annoyed that Ikenga did not show up at the farm and intends scolding him. Surprisingly however, he finds Olachi rolling on the floor, lamenting.

IFEUWABUNIKE: [*Alarmed*]. *Hei!* What is happening? [*Drops his farm tools and gets hold of Olachi*] What has come over you? You want to kill yourself?

Louder wailing is the answer he got. Ifeuwabunike lifts her and place her on a chair.

OLACHI: [*Raising her hands*]. I am finished. My enemies have triumphed over me. They have succeeded in sending me empty-handed to the grave.

IFEUWABUNIKE: Which enemies? Stop shouting and tell me what the matter is.

Pronouncing doom on your self is not good.

OLACHI: Alright. You want to hear what happened, isn't it? Okay [*Trying to control herself*]. Ikenga, *otu nkpuru anya nji ahu uzo* has ran away.

IFEUWABUNIKE: What! When? Where? Why?

OLACHI: [*Weeping*]. He found out that you are not his real father and here   is not his home.

IFEUWABUNIKE: Oh, what an ill fortune. [*Shakes his head*]. But how did he know?

OLACHI: Opuruiche and her sons.

IFEUWABUNIKE: [*Melancholic*]. When will this devil of a woman stop causing havoc in my life and in my family? This was how she   envied and quarreled with Adaugo when she was pregnant till she died. Now she has made Ikenga run away. She will never know peace. [*Turns to Olachi*]. When did he leave?

OLACHI: Not too long ago.

Ifeuwabunike dashes out in quest of Ikenga. He goes round the town, asking almost every person he meets on the way if he or she saw Ikenga. For many who don't him, he described Ikenga's physique. He also went to some houses and asked the occupants if Ikenga visited. But none answered in the affirmative.

Ifeuwabunike continued the search till twilight without success. Then he returns like a hunter whose many traps caught no prey. He enters lifelessly and meets Olachi who has cried her royal voice raucous.

OLACHI: [*Curiously*]. Did you find him?
IFEUWABUNIKE: [*Exhausted*]. No trace.

Olachi continues from where she stopped, calling the name of his husband.

IFEUWABUNIKE: Please stop crying. I believe he will come back. It is only a foolish   child that will abandon his mother that carried him for good nine months in the womb, and nurtured him to adulthood. [*Holding her*]. Get up. Let's go inside. I am certain he will return. Don't bother yourself.

Olachi stands reluctantly and enters inside with Ifeuwabunike. She couldn't sleep. It was a night of nightmare for her.

SCENE 4

Ikenga can now be hardly recognized. He is now a wanderer to the core, stinking vagabond and lonely rover in an unknown land. Even a blind man, need not a Seer to tell his predicament. His sordid countenance exudes repulsive odour, echoes a traveller and reechoes a renegade. Nonetheless, the ghetto boy seems determined to continue his journey to unknown destination.

But at a point, he gets tired of rambling. Fell on the ground, facing the blue sky; stares at it as if asking the firmaments, where do I go from here? Takes a second thought of his plight and decides to return like the prodigal son. For his appetite has consumed all he had, including the bean cakes he bought with the last two cowries his hitherto father gave him, but a big problem surfaces. He no longer recognizes the way he came from.

Ikenga then resolves once more to continue his journey fatefully and faithfully. He stands to continue, but falls. His spirit was willing but the flesh weak. His body needs thorough rest.

He stands again and did not fall this time. His will power seems to have adapted and amassed vigour to accomplish his resolution. He was now determined than ever before not to return to his retch. He trekked and trekked, traipsing up and down hill and valleys for days. At night, branches of trees became his bed. Wet by rain and dried by sun. What a wearisome journey!

As he journeyed, miles away he hears human voices and gladly hastens to the scene. When he got there, it became a graveyard, and all eyes were on him. The girls of the town, Ikpa, ceased playing their cat's cradle and gaze at him as if he has committed a heinous crime. But his offence was the filthy nature of his appearance.

Being ashamed, he runs to the secluded area of the town. Not too long after, he was stopped by a middle-aged macho man.

COMMANDER: *Hey boy!* Stop there. Where are you going?

IKENGA: [*Lifelessly*]. I don't know Sir. I have been traveling for the past six days without a destination.

COMMANDER: That's interesting.

IKENGA: Please give me water to drink.

COMMANDER: Do I look like a sailor or a fisherman?

IKENGA: Please Sir, I am very thirsty.

Commander suspects him to be a spy. But after considering his unkempt hair, shaggy beard, worn out clothes, disfigured morocco shoes and offensive smell, apparently believed his story.

COMMANDER: [*Calls*]. Onuma.

Immediately a lanky figure wearing a frizz hairdo comes out from the nearby shack.

ONUMA: [*Bows*]. Yes Commander, at your service.

COMMANDER: Get this traveller, water to drink.

Onuma returns to the cabin he came out from.

IKENGA: You are a Commander?

COMMANDER: Just as you heard.

IKENGA: [*Curious*]. Commander who? Of what?

COMMANDER: [*Irritated*]. Don't ask questions boy. Just call me Commander, okay?

IKENGA: [*Frightened*]. Yes Sir, yes Commander.

Onuma brings a cup of water. Ikenga collects it and drinks like a man who received a gunshot. After emptying the cup, he returns it. Though not satiated, he was grateful.

COMMANDER: [*To Ikenga*]. You said you have no destination?

IKENGA: Yes Commander.

COMMANDER: Would you stay with us?

IKENGA: I have no choice.

COMMANDER: May be. [*Turns to Onuma*].
Take him inside.

IKENGA: Thank you Commander.

At midnight, Ikenga sensed a tap and
wakes in fear.

COMMANDER: Just be calm boy. Did Onuma
tell you anything?

IKENGA: Yes. About safeguarding –

COMMANDER: [*Interrupts*]. Then why are you
sleeping?

IKENGA: I pleaded with him and he agreed
that I start on the first market day that
is two days ahead. [*Brief pause*]. He said
the door shouldn't be opened.

COMMANDER: [*Sharply*]. Yes.

IKENGA: Why?

COMMANDER: Just do as you are instructed.
Goodbye.

Ikenga is left swimming in an ocean of
turbulent waves coupled with emotional
trauma.

IKENGA: [*Recalls*]. Just do as you're instructed. I wonder what is inside there. Hidden treasures? A kidnapped child? Ritual objects? [*Gives up pondering and remembers Utogidi*]. I will never return there till I find my father's land.

This recollection seems to have increased his melancholic mood. He remains silent for a while and continues his interrupted night voyage.

SCENE 5

On the scheduled *Orie* day, Ikenga is stationed at the outer door of the shanty in lieu of the inner as earlier instructed. The change was due the perceived risk of placing a new comer in front of the sacred room.

The door squeaks behind Ikenga and Onuma emerges with a plate of exiguous meal.

ONUMA: Here is your food. [*Drops it on the floor*].

IKENGA: Thanks. [Onuma walks inside]. Wait. [Onuma turns back]. What of Commander? I haven't seen him for two days now.

ONUMA: He travelled with his entourage.

IKENGA: His entourage?

ONUMA: Yes.

IKENGA: To where?

ONUMA: I know not. Just eat your food. [*Returns to his duty post*].

Ikenga was not happy with the way Onuma responded. He perhaps has more questions to ask but could not help it. As he is doing justice to the food, he hears a squawk and jerks up as if in an elevator seat. He tiptoes inside and finds Onuma's lifeless with his mouth frothy. Eyes mysteriously open, gushing blood fitfully.

With the food beside Onuma, Ikenga suspects poison and shouts helplessly for help. He suddenly stands attentively examining his body, for he has eaten same food. But why would Onuma poison himself?

This he ponders and rules out toxin as the cause of Onuma's death. More also as he hasn't experienced any gastrointestinal reactions.

As he was trying to solve the puzzle of Onuma's mysterious demise, strange solemn sounds emanate from the prohibited room. He looks on with dread as the door slowly opens telekinetically. Inside the room was a preternatural figurine. He catches a vague glimpse and retreats. The crimson goggled eyes and sheen of the statue raised Ikenga's heels above his head.

IKENGA: Arusi, arusi-a-a-a-a-a-a-a-a-a. [*Vociferates as he runs away from   the horrific scene*].

Ikenga later halts, breathing in and out heavily. He is baffled and couldn't apprehend the fatal incident. However, as he trudges and broods, it dawns on him that that strange statuette must be responsible for Onuma's death.

SCENE 6

Ikenga continues wandering, this time with nothing. He gets to a place where he hears lamentations. He hurries as fast as his legs could go to the sight.

When he got there, all eyes were on him, this time not with disdain but with deference. Though he was hungry, he looked more nourished and neat than them. In fact, he can count the ribs of the fattest person among them.

Ikenga walks aside to a lanky lad to inquire what is responsible for this pathetic state. The boy is an orphan, the last child of *Ichie* Onuoha. His seven siblings and parents lost their lives to famine and epidemic that plagues Umuezeka. Some of his elder brothers were among those who went to recover *arusi-odum* and did not return. Some others including his sisters died of infectious diseases. But he is still alive.

IKENGA: Who are these people?
DEBE: We are the people of Umuezeka.

IKENGA: Why are you all seated her and crying to death? What is the   matter?

DEBE: [*Finds it difficult to talk*]. Hunger and pestilence.

IKENGA: Why? Can't these young men and women farm? Or are there no medicinal herbs and vegetables to cure illnesses?

DEBE: The soil has defied our strength. You can rarely find a healthy green leaf here.

IKENGA: What! Something must be wrong then.

DEBE: [*Slowly*]. Our chief god was taken away from us.

IKENGA: You mean the head god of this land was stolen?

DEBE: [*Unhappy*]. Yes. *Arusi-odum*, our god of life and defense.

IKENGA: How come?

DEBE: We don't know. All we know is that the thieves reside at the outskirts of a land called Ikpa.

IKENGA: Ikpa?

DEBE: Yes.

Gradually, it dawns on Ikenga that that figure at Commander's hut must be the very *arusi* these dying people seek for.

IKENGA: So, that is it. [*Nodding his head in comprehension*].
DEBE: What is it?
IKENGA: [*Ignores the question*]. But since you people know where your *arusi* is, why didn't the able bodied youth go and rescue it.
DEBE: All those who went in turns to reclaim it including four of my brothers, never returned alive.
IKENGA: My goodness! [*Angry*]. He must be very wicked and those who live by the sword die by it.
DEBE: Who?

Ikenga leaves Debe and walks boldly to the front of the minute crowd.

IKENGA: [*Loudly*]. I can help. I will go and bring back *arusi-odum*.

Some who closed their eyes praying for death, sit up. They stare at him improbably. If only they had the strength, he would be made a laughing stock.

IKENGA: I can do it for you. Just give me your blessings and have faith.

Ichie Ononanukume walks towards him torpidly with a third leg, desiring a fourth one. He is being tortured by ill health.

ONONANUKUME: My son you want to tread where serpents don't. What you want to do has claimed the lives of virtually all our youths. Just look around you and see. [*Waving his hand sideways*] Stronger and older men than you have tried but never lived to tell the story. Those who stole our god are not stronger or more in number than us, but have defeated us because *arusi-odum* is against us. He is angry for us because of the King's evil act including subversion of an ancient tradition. So, we have accepted our fate.

IKENGA: I don't believe in fate. I believe in self-determination. You can work out your freedom and success.

AKUBUIKE: [*Comes out*]. Indeed, you speak out of youthful exuberance. But experience remains the better teacher.

IKENGA: If experience is the better teacher, then let me learn also.

OKWUDIRI: [*Moves closer to Ikenga*]. I can see you are a foolhardy fellow. However young man, this is a case of life and death. Do you want to die?

IKENGA: If it will save these dying souls, yes, but if not, no. I am not afraid of death. I am only afraid of living like a dead man.

ONONAKUME: You seem to be wise and brave. And it seems you like adventure. But I want to let you know that what thrills, kills. What an elder sit and see, if the young climbs to the top of a tree, he won't see it. Moreover, you are a stranger. We don't want you to die for our sins. If really *arusi-odum* is a true god, let him fight for himself and us. So, go thy way.

IKENGA: Nay. Let your sins be upon me.

All marvel at his profound resolve and bravery. *A stranger, willing and ready to sacrifice his life for us?* What is the motivation? Puzzling indeed!

They wonder and ponder in abject obscurity. In fact some think he is psycho or one of their enemies sent to make a serious caricature of their predicament. However when all dissuasions proved abortive, they reluctantly let him take the deadly risk. *Since he wishes to be one the novel martyrs of Umuezeka, so be it.*

As he is about to leave, Omenala appears with a black cock. The people, including the elders who go to his abode in the thick forest to consult him, are surprised to see him again after he made his public appearance during the celebration of the imprisoned King's baby.

OMENALA: Wait my son. [*Moves close to Ikenga and hesitates. Then stands at arm's length*]. Kneel. [*Ikenga obeys*].
OMENALA: You have a very tedious task ahead, but the possibility of every task,

whether tedious or trivial depends on the individual's state of mind. If you are fearful, you will fail, but if you are confident, you will succeed. [*Omenala taps the cock on his chest thrice and circles it round his head same number of times. He gives him a dry kola nut, a scarlet cloth and black powdery substance wrapped in umu leaf*].
When you get there, do not look at the image. Enter with your back and place the kola nut in front of it, behind you. Then rub the powdery substance on your palms, and cover the image with the cloth before you turn to carry. You can now go, we await your return. [*Ikenga stands in fine fettle*]. Remember, only those who chant songs of life, even at the point of death, succeed in life.

Ikenga trots out gamely.

DEBE: [*Shouts*]. Wait. [Ikenga halts. He b*rings out a sword and walks to him*]. My father gave this [raises the sword] to his third son before he died. The first and second died before him at Ikpa. The third, and fourth also died there. The fifth, two sisters and mother died here. My father when he was giving this sword to our third son before he died, said as long as a freeborn holds this sword, there is hope for Umuezeka.

So before our third son went to Ikpa, he gave the sword to the fourth, the fourth to the fifth. This they did due to fear of dying with it at Ikpa, and quench the light of Umuezeka. Now I am holding it. And before I die, I must give it to someone else to keep alive the hope of Umuezeka. But I have been thinking that if my elder brothers went to Ikpa with this sword, they may have succeeded or at least returned alive.

IKENGA: [*Knowing his probable subsequent statement*]. But I am not a freeborn of Umuezeka.

DEBE: Yes, but for taking our problem as yours and deciding to die for us,   you are now one of us.

IKENGA: [*Encouraged. Collects the sword*]. I owe you nothing but to return this sword to you and your people. [*Exit*].

Umuezeka is in a moribund state. Since Ezeilo sent away his sacrificial son, she has known no joy. The people have experienced scourge after scourge, culminating to loss of lives. The Babel of ill fortune has swept away many especially children who have lesser threshold to withstand drought and pestilence. The situation is so alarming that census can be adequately taken in Umuezeka by one enumerator within minutes.

Dead bodies and animals lie all over the land unburied and stinking. Those still alive, wish death. From the severity, if the famine and epidemic continue, some may turn to rapacious cannibals as the only way to survive.

Ichie Onuoha and *Ichie* Udokasi died of ill health and grief for the death of their children, while *Nze* Eluwa committed suicide when his only two sons died in quest of *arusi-odum*.

Surprisingly however, Ezeilo who is in prison and the cause of their predicament is still alive and appears healthier than all of them excluding the Agunu Chief Priest.

SCENE 7

The degenerating remnants of Umuezeka sit on the ground hopelessly and hellishly. They are speechless and motionless. The young girls' previously velvety hairs have become ratty. Ikenga seems to be their only recourse and last bastion of hope.

Omenala is of no succour as without *arusi-odum* he is handicap. Notwithstanding, he does not appear famish.

As they sit and some lie like living corpses, Ikenga appears like a guardian angel. They are dumfounded, seeing the achievement in his trembling hands; more also without strain and within so short a time. What a wave of magic hand!

Ikenga became a demigod to them. The people of Umuezeka see him as an extra-ordinary being – a saviour sent by their ancestors.

He didn't waste time in search of *arusi-odum*, which he believed to be the effigy inside the forbidden room at Ikpa. Fortunately also, no guard was present except sleeping Onuma. So without any resistance, he performed the rites and ran out with it. It was indeed a marvelous success without stress.

The people being dumbstruck by impossibility made possible; stood in awe, looking like idiots. Recovering from the joy shock, they dance feebly round Ikenga, both old and young. In unison, they render a period of panegyric. Ikenga's brave accomplishment improved their health psychologically. Glad tidings run through Umuezeka and environs. So much so that some neighbouring towns that earlier declared Umuezeka a wilderness came to see the reason for the jubilation.

Everybody is happy and joyful, except Omenala who portrays uncommon indifference. He passes through the circle of townspeople dancing. Collects *arusi-odum* from Ikenga, looks at him and shakes his head dismayingly. Then he walks to the wind, engross with telepathic communication without congratulating or appreciating Ikenga for the lethal job well done.

Ikenga felt uneasy at first but is carried away by the praises showered on him by the people. They embrace him warmly with tears of joy and shake his hand with reverence.

The elders out of great joy and veneration want to crown him King there and then but *Nze* Okwudiri called *Ichie* Ononankume's attention to their praxis of no royal road to royalty.

As Ikenga receives eulogies and adoration, Okwudiri makes his case to fellow elders at a corner.

OKWUDIRI: What you want to do is not in accord with the tradition of our land. Moreover, that boy is a stranger.

ONONANKUME: [*Rejuvenated and happy*]. But he has done more than us the indigenes. He has risked his life and saved us from extinction. Umuezeka, which used to be the pride and helper of her neighbours was abandoned and about to be wiped out from the earth, yet none including our brother, Umuokaka showed compassion. But this young man who you call a stranger sacrificed his life for us, for a people he knows not, for strangers equally. And according to our receptive custom, he is entitled to the highest position of honour in our land. More also none of us presently is brave enough to be King like him, or are you interested.

OKWUDIRI: No. I agree with all you have said, but our custom also demands that one who is not of the royal lineage can only become a King on two conditions. One, if the incumbent King does not have a male child.

ONONANKUME: Yes. We don't know where Ezeilo exiled his son. And even if we know, he is to be sacrificed. So it is as good as not having a male child.

OKWUDIRI: And two, he must defeat the incumbent King in a bloody combat except the King is dead or surrenders.

AKUBUIKE: That is true. We shouldn't create any loophole now that we are just still at the bank of the sea. [*Warns*]. Posterity will not forgive us.

ONONANKUME: Well, I did not want to subject Ezeilo to a painful and disgraceful death, because I know he will be no match for such a young, energetic and fearless man who has done what hundreds of men couldn't. However, I will not be the one to alter the traditions of Umuezeka, knowing its grave consequences. So let it be as you say.

Ikenga, who is enraptured by the fun he is having with the people is called aside and acquainted with the development. He stands, reminisces his severe experience, how he vowed not to return to Utogidi, until he finds his father. He shakes his head as if shaking off a spell.

IKENGA: It may be, the gods want to reward me for carrying the cross of your people. But if it be not so, let me die a hero.

The elders are touched. They proceed to inform Ezeilo who is now more or less a curmudgeon. When notified of the situation, he starts seething, moving around like a caged hungry tiger and swears not to live and see another, except his son, rule in his kingdom not to talk of a stranger. Consequently, he is released from the stinking cell to defend his throne. For a royal who eats the food of commoners and presently starving, one wonders where he got strength to bounce about, not to talk of to fight.

As the royal combat is about to start, the people are crestfallen. They deplore it, viewing it as unfair to subject Ikenga to such deadly contest, after risking his life for them. They oppose it but tradition must prevail.

The arena is set as the people form a vicious circle round Ezeilo and Ikenga. Some like Debe after collecting his father's sword refuse to watch. Townspeople misprize Ezeilo, casting their votes for Ikenga.

Ononankume hands Ezeilo's sword back to him, while Okwudiri spares Ikenga his sword with words of motivation. Everybody was on Ikenga's side. No single soul wants Ezeilo alive.

Ezeilo looks fraught and bad tempered. Ikenga appears calm but pernicious. Both move opposite each other in the bloody court with the sole intent to kill.

EZEILO: So you are the reason for this jubilation. How am I sure you are not the Commander or one of his men?

IKENGA: So you know him? Then your hands are not clean.

EZEILO: Don't pretend to be innocent, boy. If not for anything, for wanting to reap where you did not sow. For wanting to kill a King and take over his Kingdom; for allowing inordinate ambition to cloud your sense of morals, you are already filthy.

IKENGA: You are entitled to your words old man. If that would be a show of appreciation by the gods for my sacrificial service, then it is not too much. And I know the gods are impartial.

EZEILO: [*Sardonic*]. Now I see that you want to build a house without counting its cost. If the gods are fair as you suppose, they won't allow you participate actively in your own death. I warn you, a kitten that wants to attack a cat dies untimely. And never in history has a rat defeated a cat.

IKENGA: [*Undaunted*]. That might as well be so. But the cat can't enter into certain holes with the rat.

EZEILO: You utter nonsense boy. Be it known to you that a carpenter, who wants to inherit a coffin maker's shop, should be prepared to see fearful faces.

IKENGA: [*Chuckles*]. How fearful? To the point of resignation, or familiarity? Indeed those who are loquacious are more often than not empty vessels.

EZEILO: That is a cheap froth. The truth is that a child that points at his father to his face dies without fingers. Likewise, he who insults old age never gets old.

IKENGA: Big lies! The old bones shall break into pieces while the young shall grow.

EZEILO: You make me laugh. If you are going to walk on thin ice, you might as well dance.

IKENGA: You only threaten and rave like a coward.

EZEILO: May be. But the slightest threat of a panther is not a mark of cowardice.

IKENGA: [*Chuckles*]. Old one, you forget that the prancing of the panther is no threat to the elephant.

EZEILO: Shut up toad. It is only cowards that relish in vain speeches. Come you greenhorn, let me show you what it means to be a warrior.

IKENGA: Just like the hunter in pursuit of an elephant does not stop throwing stones at birds, here I am. [*Roared intrepidly*].

The combat commences. It was a sheer clash of titans. Attacking and defending; they strategically employ their gladiatorial skills. It is obviously iron to iron. Ikenga now have an edge over his opponent as he bleeds his right leg.

OKWUDIRI: [*With more than a hint of sarcasm, whispers to Nze Akubuike*]. I know he cannot withstand such a fire of fresh blood.

In fury, Ezeilo assails Ikenga and left blood trickling from his left elbow. A recess was mutually initiated at this juncture.

EZEILO: When the hunter shoots without missing, the birds fly without perching. You can now see that a warrior is always a warrior. Young or old, free or imprisoned, well fed or starved.

IKENGA: [*Determined*]. The son of a warrior is always one too.

EZEILO: [*Laughs*]. I warn you; a child who uncovers his father's nakedness either becomes blind or remains cursed all the days of his life.

IKENGA: A man who robs a lad robes, will have no one to clothe him, when he walks with three legs.

EZEILO: Let me warn you, the river does not flow through the forest without bringing down trees.

IKENGA: And no tree is big enough to disrespect the wind, rather they bow when it blows.

EZEILO: Hmn, he who grows long teeth should have long lips to cover them.

IKENGA: The man, who raises a child's corn high above his head, will certainly drop it when his hand loses strength.

EZEILO: *Hnm,* I warn you again. A child that challenges his father does not bury him.

IKENGA: Neither is it customary for a father to bury his son. A man, who wrongs a child, dies without heir. [*Vexed*]. And may your mouth speak words no more.

EZEILO: The rant of a rat.

Ikenga angrily charges towards Ezeilo, intending to thrust his stomach through, but his sword falls. Yet he stylishly throws him to the ground. Ezeilo is on the ground while Ikenga is on top of him.

Using his left knee, Ikenga arrests Ezeilo's right hand with which he holds his sword. And with his left hand, he presses Ezeilo's neck. Ezeilo struggles fruitlessly to free himself from Ikenga's grip.

Having seized Ezeilo, he stretches forth his right hand to pick his sword and end the duel. The people look forward to his victory. But as he stretches to get his weapon, he creates a leeway for Ezeilo who frees his right hand and impales his side. Ikenga slowly slumps.

The people shout in sorrow. They can't believe their eyes. They wail for Ikenga. *Why should the gods allow a man that saved them from annihilation, to be killed by another who caused their predicament?* They hate Ezeilo the more for putting Ikenga to the sword. Many prayed *arusi-odum* to resuscitate Ikenga and strike Ezeilo dead, but they were disappointed like the prophets of Baal.

Ezeilo draws out his sword from Ikenga's side and spits on his face in triumph, but something traumatic happens. Ezeilo notices streak scars at Ikenga's temple and recoils to the bewilderment of the spectators. He slowly comes back. Buries the tip of his sword, tears Ikenga's sheep-skin shirt and visible to his goggled eyes is a necklace similar to that he gave his son about twenty-four years ago. The son whom in the bid to save his life sent him away; is now lying lifeless before him; killed by the same man who sacrificed all to save him. Piece by piece, it dawns on him that that the young man lying unconscious in front of him is his son, Ikenga.

Ezeilo is motionless and tremendously grieved. He wished it was a dream. He wanted the hand of time tick backward. He wished he surrendered. He wished he was never a King. He even wished he was not born or fathered a son. Unfortunately, his wishes were not horses.

EZEILO: [*Kneels, holding Ikenga*]. Ikenga-a-a-a-a-a-a-a-a. [*Shouts in agony*]. It is I, Ezeilo, your father. Wake up, get up and take your throne. Let me die instead. Wake up Ike-nga-a-a-a-a-a-a-a-a. [*Weeps sour*].

Omenala approaches slowly. Ezeilo faces him.

EZEILO: [*Looks at Omenala murderously*]. So, this is what the prophecy is all about. Have I done any wrong by leading my people? Is it a crime that I continued from where my father stopped? Or have I done evil by bringing a Prince into the world, to continue from where I will stop? Are the gods so heartless and irrational to unleash this eternal wickedness on me and my lineage? [*Shakes his head in despair*].

In vain have I tried to avert the prophecy of the gods. In futility I have tried to save my son, my only son. To naught did I eliminate Umuezeka warriors, all in the bid to kill the foretold murderer of my son. Not knowing that the man I sought is my very self. [Weeps]. I believed the gods and their priests. But look at where my belief has landed me. I strongly believed strange gods that has mouth but utter not a word; have legs but move not except when carried, and was captured but couldn't save itself. Oh! Look at how this has influenced my actions to the fulfillment of a devilish divination. Now, I am a victim of fake belief.

[*Recalls ruefully*]. The child will be brave but will be killed by a strong man who does not want him to be King. [*Points at Omenala*]. You said so. You pronounced that destiny. But how on earth would I not want my son to be King? Which right thinking being would say I don't want my son, Ikenga to become *Igwe* of Umuezeka? Which King would not want his son to take over from him? Which leader would not hand over power? Will he rule forever? Will he live forever? Is the throne eternally made for a man? [*Shouts*]. Tell me Omenala. Tell me, you messenger of lies.

Omenela is filled with indignation, but like his god, did not speak.

EZEILO: Though they say, 'O king live forever'. I, just like every other King knows that no King on earth lives forever. No mortal does. If I won't live forever, then it is certain that I will definitely hand over the staff of Kingship. And if I will as a matter of must leave the throne one day for someone else, is it not natural and a pleasure that I transfer the authority to my own son, which our tradition also enjoins. Answer me. [*To Omenala*] Speak to me. Or has your dummy god made you dumb? You doomed prophet of doom!

How will I not want him to become King, if I knew he was my son? Did you expect me to allow a supposed stranger become King of Umuezeka, while I am still alive? If you were in my shoes you will do as I did, as our tradition supports. That is why I accepted the challenge. That was why I killed him. I never knew he was my son, my blood, my only son.

Our tradition and you made me believe in destiny, but now I know that the so-called destiny is in one's hands, in our hands. Yes, in my hands. [Shakes his head and grinds his teeth terrifically]. No! No it can be. Nay! Never!

In sad perspective of woes, he took his sword and made a channel through his stomach. Tremendous fear falls on the people and they run helter-skelter, away from the bloodcurdling scene. The elders are sorrowfully shocked but did not move an inch. They were held spell bound by the tragic death of Ezeilo and his son.

SCENE 8

Right now at Utogidi, Olachi is returning from Nwagwazi stream. At the T-junction, her calabash falls from her head, as she is about to fasten her loose wrapper.

She is unhappy. First, for the calabash that shattered into irreparable smithereens. And for the distance she would cover to fetch the water again, that is, if she finds someone who will be kind enough to lend her a gourd. The distance though not far, gave her great concern because she is becoming aged, cantankerous too.

Olachi reflects on the mishap as she goes home. Never has her calabash fallen since she started fetching water lately at Utogidi. And now it fell, it occurred at a junction that connects three roads. This she perceives to be ominous. She remembers her uncle, Ifeuwabunike and hopes all is well.

On her way, she meets two women discussing the gory news of royal demise in Umuezeka, which is being transmitted near and far. The women are returning from Afor market and are right in front of her. She picks interest and listens, walking quietly behind them.

The women are discussing loudly. At the mention of the King unknowingly killing his son and committed suicide thereafter, Olachi heart sinks. She thinks of it briefly; thinks of Ezeilo, Ikenga, her shattered calabash, and shouts, then faints.

Out of fear, the women threw away their bags and baskets, and run in opposite direction inside the bush. They later came out from their hiding places and saw Olachi lying on the ground motionless.

They became confused, wondering what caused the sudden syncope. They move towards Olachi to help her. On getting there, one of them places her ear on Olachi's bosom and shouts. The other woman runs away but later comes back and did what the first has done and both shout for help. But no one is forth coming because where they are is isolated.

One of the women tries to revive her by pressing her chest. When it didn't pay off, she employs mouth-to-mouth restitution, but Olachi did not respond either.

The other woman then runs to her bag, brings a bottle of water and sprinkles it on Olachi's face. The water only drizzled down like that poured on the back of a duck. Olachi has kicked the bucket.

THE END.

GLOSSARY

A

Afo-nkwu – Stomach filled with wine.

Agbonma – A legendary beautiful woman who refused to marry. She was so beautiful that even young men begged for her hand in marriage even when she has reached menopause.

Aru – Abomination.

Arusi-Odum – The chief god (a statue) in the land of Umuezeka which
literally means god of lion.

E

Eligwe – Heaven

I

Ichies and Nzes – Titled men in Igbo land.

Isea – So be it. It is used to express affirmation or agreement to a statement.

N

Ngwa – A commanding word for one to do something.

Nkenke ehi na chu igwe-ehi oso – Small elephant that chases groups of elephants away.

Nne – Mother

Nnhu. Ugbua ka ibiara – Yes. Now you have come. In other words, one has done what is expected.

Nwa oma, ebubedike, nwa ge je mgba, onye ga achi obodo Umuezeka – Good child, strong man, child that will go places, one who will rule the land of Umuezeka.

O

Obi – The King's palace or reception hall.

Obizi – Is the longest and purest river in Umuezeka.

Ofia Ekabo – An evil forest in the outskirts of Umuezeka, where rejected and abominable persons/animals are buried.

Ohu – Slave or slavery.

Oji Eze di Eze na aka – The King's Kola nut is with him.

Orie, Afor, Nkwo, Eke – Four market days in Igbo land

Otu nkpuru anya nji ahu uzo – An Igbo proverb that contextually means my only child but literally means only one eye with which I see.

U

Umuada – Daughters of a particular village.